YOU CAN'T MAKE OLD FRIENDS

A novel by

TOM TROTT

Brighton's No.1 Private Detective

You Can't Make Old Friends
Choose Your Parents Wisely
It Never Goes Away

Other books by Tom Trott

The Benevolent Dictator

Second edition

Copyright © 2016 Thomas J Trott

Cover design & illustration by Thomas Walker

ISBN: 1540745732
ISBN-13: 978-1540745736

for Nick, Simon, Joel, Tony, Will,
George, Prash, and Matt,
my Rorys

PROLOGUE

IN YOUR HOUSE, your flat, or your cardboard box, there is a cupboard. You know the cupboard I mean. Somewhere to put all the things you don't want to see. The things you don't have space for anymore. The broken things you can't bring yourself to throw away. At the back of your memory there is a cupboard too.

And just like in your house, your flat, or your cardboard box, if you put too much in there, you can't close the door anymore...

Two boys scampered through the woods. Crunching on twigs. Swinging on branches. The mud kicking up onto their clothes.

The sun was streaming through gaps in the trees, lighting rays of dust that, when you are moving at speed, flicker and dance like a zoetrope in the corner of your eye.

They ducked under bushes, skipped over tree stumps,

at lightning speed, following a well-worn path. The bigger of the two leading the way through cobwebs, over anthills.

Soon clouds began to cover the sun, the rays of dust giving way to dim shadows and damp moss. Then it started to rain. First in small spots. Then a deluge. Although already drenched, they had made it just in time.

The larger boy pulled back the canopy wall and they sheltered inside. Mud smeared. Dripping wet. Together they huddled by the tree stump that marked their den. And on it their sign:

Shivering, the bigger boy decided to wring out his clothes, so he peeled off his once-white polo shirt. As he did so the other noticed something: his chest was... different. He reached out a hand to feel, running his fingers over the ribs. It felt different too.

Footsteps! Crunching, splashing footsteps announced the presence of others. They can't have found this place! Not this place, their last refuge!

Three bigger boys ripped apart the den. The rain and the mud flowed in. The smaller boy ran to defend the first but he was batted to the ground like an errant football.

He could only lie there, winded, whilst they started pummelling his friend. He closed his eyes, he didn't want to watch. But he could always hear it. Always.

Even today...

I Always Knew I'd Find You Dead One Day

SHIT. So I had slept in my office again. In my chair. In the same clothes. For the second night in a row. I smelled like a tramp.

I could hear a bin van. Birdsong. It must have been early. What business did I have being awake this early? It wasn't like me.

My desk was experiencing a minor earthquake. I thought that was odd until I realised it was just my phone vibrating. *That must be why I'm awake.* I fished for it underneath yesterday's Chinese takeaway tubs. Or were they the day before's? Either way I needed to leave the office.

It was a text, not that my phone could do anything more than texts and calls, and it was terse:

"The beach. Now."

I didn't have their number in my phone, hopefully

they knew my business. Normally I wouldn't respond to such a summoning, but I really needed to get out.

The morning sun was spitting rays of dust through the blinds, and by this half-light I did the best I could with the dying electric razor that I kept in my desk. Nothing I could do about the smell though.

The beach? To someone from Brighton that usually means the area between the two piers: the Palace Pier and the wreck of the West Pier. Or more realistically, wherever you can get a spot. I've been on the beach at two a.m. and found it just as packed as during the day. Full of people lighting pointless disposable barbecues and pouring vodka into a watermelon for no good reason.

As I rode down through a sea-mist on my old Honda I prayed that there wouldn't be a crowd, I wasn't in the mood to be looked at by anyone. Wondering if the beach would be busy at this time, especially in this weather, I realised that I had absolutely no idea what the time was, and on a grey day like this there was no sun to give me a clue.

The Palace Pier emerged out of the mist as I approached the seafront. I still call it the Palace Pier despite it being renamed years ago. Brightonians either call it the Palace Pier or just The Pier, but never, ever Brighton Pier.

It is now the only pier, but there had been three for one brief moment back in the reign of Queen Victoria.

The first was The Royal Suspension Chain Pier, but that was prematurely destroyed by a storm in 1896. It was already scheduled for demolition, having been outshone by the West Pier. "The West Pier is the best pier" people used to say, and I always wished I could have seen it in its heyday. There was a concert hall for heaven's sake. There was also a magician and escapologist called The Great Omani who used to be tied in chains and thrown off the end into the water. When this was no longer exciting enough, petrol was added and the waves set ablaze. Apparently, one night Worthing Pier called up to warn them that the West Pier was on fire. They were about forty years too early.

They say it was arson. It still stung me that someone would burn down a piece of history. A great piece of history. All that left was the Palace Pier, and that's just for tourists.

When I got to the seafront and cruised along Madeira Drive, I could see that the beach was as busy as my place on a Saturday night. That is to say empty. Empty as a politician's promise. Empty as Barbie's knickers.

I could see only one group on the beach, a couple of hundred metres east of the pier. I parked up next to a small smattering of cars, by the statue of Steve Ovett, and took a look.

A cold, wet winter always strips the city back to its foundations. And so much of the city's reputation is surface. The clubbers, the Pride marchers, the eco-warriors are all summer creatures. In the winter the city is just another grey, miserable seaside town like all the others. The same shut-up shops, the same graffiti, the same kids. The same neighbourhoods you avoid, the same streets you don't walk down at night. The same problems. Sure, Brighton is paradise, if you're white, middle class, and were born before 1980. Maybe that's being too harsh. Sometimes you can get away with just two of those.

As I stepped over the old Volks Electric Railway line I got my first view. *Well, well, well... look who wants me back*, I thought. I could see the unmistakable high-vis jackets of uniformed police officers. High-vis that seemed especially pointless standing in the middle of an empty beach. It could be a lollypop lady convention.

They were right by where the Chain Pier would have been. And as I crunched onto the pebbles, stepping over strands of dead, black seaweed, I could make out CSI men in coveralls, which must mean a body. Or at least a body part. That would explain the group of seagulls hovering above their heads. Not even flapping their wings, just riding the wind.

Even with the mist, the sea this morning was shimmering enticingly. I often have the urge to just dive in and swim to France for the afternoon, but apparently it isn't that easy. Maybe I could make it just as far as that fishing boat or something or other on the horizon. They say the horizon is about three miles if you're standing at sea level. I could make that. I could definitely make that. But there were police waiting for me.

As the only person for what seemed like miles around, I hit their radar pretty fast. And then I saw George, wearing high-vis and one of those ridiculous shower-cap things that uniformed officers wear when it's raining to keep their silly hats dry.

'Morning,' he called.

I just nodded. This was enough for the officer on guard to let me through the cordon. The CSI guys were taking photos. It made me laugh to see them still in coveralls, even with the little covers they put over their shoes, despite them being on the beach. They're not supposed to disturb the crime scene of course, but the tide was doing it regardless of their best efforts. George said something to them and they were persuaded to take a break. This gave me my first real look at it.

There it was: a naked, bloated body. Pale white, glossy like ivory, streaked with a coppery green. A man was about all I could tell. Poor bastard. George gave me a running commentary whilst I tried not to gag. I've seen worse, believe me, but when it's that early in the morning and all you have in your stomach is yesterday's Chinese it's a bit more difficult.

'Washed up this morning. Been in the water about

three days, best guess.'

'Best guess?' I asked.

'Well, the doctor's not here yet so that's coming from these guys,' he looked toward the CSI men all taking a fag break, 'but they've seen enough of these to be reliable.'

'What about his face?'

'Some kind of acid, they think.'

My mind reeled. It was just a lumpy red mass.

'Post-mortem,' he added. Thank god for that.

I looked down at the hands. I almost went again: his fingers were all missing.

'Fingers are seagull food by now.'

I don't think George had any idea how close to vomiting I was when he said that. And the constant screaming of seagulls in my ears didn't help. They were waiting for us to leave so that they could have the body. Vultures have nothing on Brighton seagulls, they'll eat your hand just to get to the chip you're holding.

It was clear by now that whoever had done this didn't want the body identified. And if they had gone to this effort you could bet his DNA wasn't in the database.

'Dental records?' I asked.

He reached down and opened the man's mouth, which wasn't what I was asking for, and I could see that he didn't have any teeth. Not anymore, anyway.

'Age?'

'About the same as you, we think.' Which was to say early thirties.

'Anything else?'

'Afraid not.'

He shrugged as if to apologise. Don't apologise, I thought. I like the difficult ones.

'This one's going to be impossible,' he said.

That's why they called *me*.

I took a step back. So what did we have? Male. Early thirties. Very long, scraggly, wild hair I could see. Sort of ginger. And his chest... I reached down, touching the cold, rubbery body. Running my hands over the ribs. I could feel... something.

It couldn't be. Could it? Various parts of my mental cortex began to fire, but I was interrupted:

'Who the fuck are you!?'

I looked up to see a sharp blonde in a tight trouser suit. It was slate grey with slight pinstriping, and very serious looking, which matched her face. Flat shoes too, which was a good thing on the pebbles. The brief sketch I got of her face was of dazzling sapphire eyes on top of pale, thin lips. Her nose had a perfect ski-slope profile to it, and her blonde hair would probably be quite stunning if it was allowed to sway and bounce seductively, but she had pulled it tight into a ponytail until it looked like it was begging to spring free. I could see she had done everything possible not to be as attractive as she was in a profession where that was still a hindrance, male or female. It was a miracle how I got away with it. That last part is of course a joke: I never got away with it.

She must have been freezing, given that she was slender and without a coat, but she didn't show it. From her introduction I got the distinct impression that she was one of those female officers who swear a lot to make up for having a vagina. And I wasn't in the mood for shouting.

'You called me,' I growled.

'*Who* called you!?'

That wasn't the reaction I was expecting. I looked to George who was straightening his silly hat and smiling like a lunatic. I understood. *Fucking hell!* I hadn't been asked back to assist a repentant and regretful police force, I was being thrown a bone by George. I didn't need charity, thank you very much.

I thought at this point I would just leave, but George proceeded to make things worse.

'This is Joe. Joe Grabarz.'

'He was touching my body,' the officer barked.

'He's a private dick.'

I knew that would piss her off, and it did. Her eyes widened and she looked like she might kill George.

He continued, 'When a case is difficult, like this, sometimes the SIO will—'

'You're telling me you call in for help?'

She got right to the point. And boy, did she make

it sound bad. A police department so devoid of good brains that they needed me to help with the tough ones. Well, not anymore. They had made that abundantly clear. Then she added a kicker:

'I decide what's difficult'.

But George didn't get what was happening, he kept going, 'This is how things work down here.'

She kicked again, 'Things don't work down here. That's why *I'm* here.'

Ouch. Then, not content to let him steal the last word, she ended the whole thing: 'Go home.'

He couldn't talk, he wasn't sure what she was saying. I wasn't sure if she was sending him home for the day, or forever. I found out later it was permanent.

'Now!' she barked. He even jumped.

And with a last forlorn look at me he started to trudge away without a word. She was impressive, in a terrifying kind of way. I took this as my cue to leave and I tried to.

'Oi, you!' meaning me, 'What did you see when you touched the body? You had that look.'

Yeah right! I thought. Like I'm going to tell you. And I said as much with my face.

I caught up with George on Madeira Drive as he was getting into his car. I had never had any idea how old he was. He usually looked not that much older than me, but I suspected he was older and just lived less than I did, until now he hadn't looked it. Now I spotted grey hairs that I hadn't before, and lines around his eyes and across his forehead. Spare skin sagged around his jowls. He looked tired and wind chafed. Then again, standing there I felt wind chafed too. He took one look at me and started talking, clearly he wanted to unload.

'Stupid bitch! Who does she think she is?'

'I don't know,' I answered honestly, 'who is she?'

'New DCI. From London.'

Wow, a DCI. That young and pretty. I shouldn't have thought pretty, I know. But I did. She can't have been that much older than me either, and looked better than I did for it. Maybe late thirties. I hadn't heard of that before.

'She's the Chief's special project,' he added.

'Who left?'

'No one yet.'

She must be special, with budgets the way they are they're looking to retire the higher-paid officers, not hire them.

'We're all on the block,' he added. He certainly was.

There didn't seem to be anything left to say so I straddled my bike. George wasn't happy with this.

'You're welcome. Probably cost me my bloody job,' he moaned.

All I could think to say was 'I didn't ask you to call me.' It was true. And I wasn't that happy with him either.

He grumbled and cursed me as he got in his car. I slipped into my helmet. Sealing off the world. With the visor down no one could see me. No one could see what I was thinking. The wind and rain, all the world, was shut away. I could close my eyes and I was anywhere. Except this time I was back in my office…

It must have been a couple of years ago, I thought. I couldn't remember every detail but I could remember Elaine's face.

She had aged wonderfully. One of those women who was nearly fifty and had managed to keep her figure the whole time. Razor sharp cheekbones that would cut you if you dared to even think about getting close.

She was sitting on her best asset, opposite my desk with a cigarette on. It wasn't in an elegant cigarette holder, but I couldn't help sketching one into my memory. She was wearing a tight pencil skirt with a slit that went to halfway up her thigh. And she had excellently toned, deep dark, lightly freckled legs. A tan obtained through years of holidays to Spain or Greece or Turkey, or wherever had the best sun-to-price-tag ratio.

I had always liked her, she was the mum you could have fun with. You could tell by the way she dyed her neat little bob a brunette shade that had just a hint of brilliant red that only showed when light from behind haloed her. It was like a secret signal to the initiated that said "I'm fun. Play with me." She wasn't her happy self anymore though, for obvious reasons.

'I've never been in your office before, Joe.'

'That's a good thing,' I said.

She fiddled with her cigarette and didn't always look at me. 'Have you heard from Rory lately?'

'No,' was all I said. It's not like you can officially announce that a friendship is dead, but she must have known. There wasn't a body, but considering it hadn't been seen for almost a decade, I'm sure any reasonable judge would issue a death certificate.

'I'm worried about him.'

She put it out there in the middle of the room as though we might both take a step back and consider it from a distance. It was for me to pick up or leave as I saw fit. Except it wasn't. If I didn't pick it up it would be forced on me soon enough and I would have to endure more painful small talk in the meantime.

'When was the last time you heard from him?' I asked.

'I don't even remember.'

'And Thalia?'

'She doesn't tell me anything.'

I was uncomfortable. I don't like having clients who know me from before. It makes me vulnerable. I can't be the cool-headed and cold-hearted bastard that the job needs. I was about to tell her there was nothing I could do, but she read it in my face before I had the chance.

'I just want to know he's ok. I ain't heard a thing from him in years!' she pleaded.

She might have been turned down a thousand times from the way her voice shook with desperation. Maybe she had. She could have been to the police. Probably had. But he wasn't really a missing person, just missing from her life, and they don't have an estranged families department.

'Mrs Sweet—' I was trying to pacify her. It didn't work.

'I ain't seen him since before his dad died. And for god's sake, Joe, don't call me Mrs Sweet. I didn't like that even when you were a kid.' She took a drag on her cigarette.

I stayed calm. 'He didn't go to the funeral?' That surprised me. Rory was an idiot sometimes, but never heartless. His own dad's funeral, I couldn't believe it.

'Neither did you.'

I didn't have a response for that. The truth was that I didn't go because I wanted to avoid just this kind of situation.

'Do it for us, Joe. For everything we did for you.'

That was a lot, for sure. But I don't like being blackmailed. Either emotionally or the real kind. So I shut her down, as lightly as I could.

'I'm sorry. Maybe if he was still my friend, or maybe if I thought he gave a shit about me I would feel inclined to help. But as it is, I'm trying to run a business here.'

'I don't have any money, Joe!'

So that's what she thought of me. Fine. I didn't care. And that was that: 'I'm sorry, Mrs Sweet.'

My Honda purred between my legs. The sea spray just managing to sneak into the gap below my helmet. The wind felt like a riot shield pushing me over.

It couldn't be Rory, could it? The age. The hair. His chest… Fuck it, I needed to be honest with myself. *I always knew I'd find you dead one day.*

2

What's Different Now?

I HEADED STRAIGHT for Gerard Street, which is amongst those terraces between London and Ditchling Roads, the poor side of London Road station. Even with Ken dead, and Rory and Thalia moved out, I doubted Elaine had moved. It was their house, through everything. Even I had lived there for a time.

I parked up and decided that I should probably now check the time if I was going to start knocking on doors. Not yet nine. But gone eight. I didn't think that was too rude. Not in the circumstances.

I knew how to find the road: the big metal dragon-fly on the side of the corner house, but I couldn't remember the number. I walked down the road, taking in each house in turn. There's that strange feeling you get when you stand in front of the right house. It's like doing one of those nursery games with the different shapes and the different holes, only with your eyes shut. You might not know which one you're picking up, but you know when it fits the hole.

Their house was narrow, and otherwise indistinguishable from the rest in the terrace if it wasn't for the purple door. I didn't even remember it had a purple door until I saw it. Then I wondered how I could forget. Then I realised that I can't have forgotten because I recognised it when I saw it. Some unsummonable memory did its job when I needed it.

It looked like nothing had changed. The purple door, the rusted railings, the ratty blinds behind the kitchen windows. Because the roads were cut into the hill, the gardens on this side of the road were a storey lower than the front of the house, giving the place a strange split layout. You entered on the middle floor where their kitchen was and Rory's bedroom had been, and went down to the living room, or up to the other bedrooms. This meant you had to climb up around five steps to reach the door.

I knocked and took a couple of steps back. I wasn't sure why, but standing there I felt like a child again. Embarrassed.

The door swung open in a bad mood. There she was, standing in a dressing gown with a cigarette stuck to her lip. The same. But very different. Haggard. Tired. Instead of smile lines now she had frown lines. And greying hair. She looked more like officer George than her former self. Not that surprising, I supposed, she had gone from a happy family to being on her own. And her son a drug dealer, absent from any of their lives. At least Thalia was all right.

I tried to start a sentence, 'Excuse me...' but she recognised me before I could get any more out.

'Joe?' She sighed, as though she had thought she would never see me again. 'Little Joe.'

'Hi, Mrs Sweet.'

If she couldn't already remember our last conversation, she could now. She looked down on me. In both ways.

'Looking for Rory?'

For the first time I could remember I struggled getting my words out, 'I don't suppose...' was all I could manage.

'Speak to Thalia.'

That was all I was going to get. This is why I hate personal cases. This is why I refused last time. I need to focus, and I can't focus when I'm trying not to hurt people. I gave a pathetic nod and stepped down to the pavement.

'What's different now?' she called as I turned my back on her.

I left that hanging in the air. I wanted to avoid saying the wrong thing. After all, I didn't *know* anything.

* * *

Where did Thalia work? It was a dry-cleaners, I was pretty sure. Somewhere off London Road. Chinese owners. Baker Street maybe.

It was. I really wasn't in the mood for politely asking if she was around so I just pushed past the owner into the back.

And there she was. Packaging up a suit. She was better looking than I remembered. When I was younger she was just Rory's little sister, but now she was undeniably a woman. Every slight imperfection had rounded out into distinctive features. And where she had been a plump girl she was now a woman with curves in all the right places. I wondered if those curves were natural or just cleverly clothed. But since she was wearing clothes, I didn't much care either way. From shoes to hair she went up, out, in, out again. And on top big round lips and big dark eyes that were staring at me, this strange man who had barged his way into the back of the shop to find her, with some concern. But then she recognised me.

'I'm looking for your brother,' was all I said. I thought straight to the point was best.

The shop owner pestered her too much for her to ask me why, but she handed me a key and gave me an address off Lewes Road. I guess looking back it was strange that she always had the key on her. But with Rory you never knew when there might be an emergency.

I rode down to the gyratory. Rory had moved into one of the new flats built out of the old garage or petrol station, or was it something else? It was something that wasn't needed any more, and homes in Brighton really were. Still are.

The new building had been a clean white box, but already pollution and dirt had stained it several shades of grey. Designed to look expensive, but done on a budget. They had Juliette balconies, I could see, one pretence to luxury. Not that I should turn my nose up, it looked a damn sight more respectable than my place.

I parked up and entered the main stairwell where I was confronted by a big, bright sign screaming "Proudly built by ABC Construction." If a sign can look smug, this one did. The carpet was the cheap, wiry kind that you expect to find in function rooms, and the stairs had those infuriating metal treads that you used to catch your school shoes on. The inside walls were white too, only they were still white and regularly cleaned. I was amazed that Rory could afford whatever the rent was here.

I went up to the third floor, the top floor, and to the second door on the right, putting my ear up against it. I didn't want to knock or call out in case there was anyone around. I didn't want to be noticed. I couldn't hear anything, not even the traffic from the street, so I slipped the key in and cautiously let the door swing open, without taking any steps. Still nothing. I crept in and quickly checked the two rooms without taking any notice of them, just making sure I was alone. I was. So I shut the door and began to take the place in.

It was a one-bedroom flat, not too dissimilar to mine in its layout. One living room with kitchenette, a bedroom, small bathroom, and in this case a separate toilet, which I found unusual in a new-build. Perhaps it was some strange holdover from the building it used to be.

What was very different was the style. Despite how small the overall floor space was it still felt sparse, and not in a cool, modernist way, more in a way that made me think Rory didn't own much. What little furnishings there were looked like they came with the place. Really, it looked like a show home. Tripod lamp. Old-style filmmaking lamp. Bare bulbs, also old-style. Scandinavian furniture. Architecture magazines that I was pretty damn sure Rory didn't read. Even art on the walls.

It didn't look like the home of a drug dealer. In fact, I would have been so sure I was in the wrong place and promptly left if it wasn't for that on the fridge was a photo of Rory and Thalia. They were smiling, which dated it back a few years. Still, I didn't have any pictures of him and those kinds of things always come in handy, so I took it. But it wasn't what I was looking for. I knew what I was looking for. Weed. Or something stronger.

I went back to the bathroom and scrubbed my hands clean, which was more a ritual before a search than it was serving any practical purpose. Then I slipped on the pair of latex gloves that I always carry with me, and started looking.

I looked in the toilet cistern first, the traditional place, but found nothing. The next obvious place was behind the bath panel. Again nothing. I was struck both times by how clean these nooks and crannies were. Either Rory didn't get up to much or he hadn't been living here long.

I moved on to the bedroom and checked first under the bed itself. Nothing there. Literally, nothing there. It was like a hotel. Although even hotels give you slippers. I checked in the wardrobe, this looked a bit more lived in. He had clothes, at least. In the top of the wardrobe he had a shoebox of photographs. They were old, and I was sure I would be in some of them, but it wasn't what I was looking for so I moved out of the bedroom to the living room and kitchenette.

Here there weren't really any hidden spaces, the cupboards were mostly bare and none of the panels were loose. The only place I thought I would hide drugs was in the extractor fan, behind the filters. It was a good idea but all I got for it was a face full of dirt. This meant it had to be the one I dreaded: under the floorboards.

Floorboards are a pain because it can be any of

them, you have to spend ages looking for the one loose one. I tried all the boards with my flick knife, another part of my essential kit, but none of them gave. I had just made it to the boards by the sofa, in the middle of the room, when pulling my knife from the gap I noticed a tiny bit of red on it. Reddish brown. Dried blood. I had seen it more than enough times to know.

I pulled out yet another essential detective's item, a black light. For those who don't know, it's an ultraviolet torch that shows up every little stain that you've tried to remove. It revealed wash marks where someone had been cleaning something up, from the middle of the room to the front door. Someone had bled a lot, and then been dragged outside. Dead or alive wasn't clear.

So it was confirmed. At least, in my mind. The body looked enough like Rory, and his flat was a crime scene. Shit. Rory, the only best friend I had ever had, dead. And not in a nice way either. In some slow way. I needed to sit down, so I slumped onto the sofa.

Another idea struck me. The sofa. Not in the cushions obviously, you would feel that, but the frame. I jumped up and with all the emotion that was boiling away inside me turned the sofa over far too easily. Neighbours would hear that.

There was a hole, I plunged my hand in and instantly felt a package. I yanked it out, ripping the hole much wider in the process. It was sealed in a black bin bag. Too heavy for weed and too light for a brick of cocaine or heroin. Not in the mood to be careful, I ripped it open and smaller bags flew everywhere.

They were small, clear bags. I picked up the nearest one and could see inside were five small, round, blue pills. Each with a tiny star debossed in the centre. I sighed a long, deep sigh, like the rush of air from an opened hangar. I knew these pills. *Rory, you dumb fuck.*

It must have been only a few months ago, although being before the police blacklisted me, it seemed far longer than that. I was hired over the phone to find a young woman.

'We just want to know she's alright,' an anxious voice trembled.

I was slowly becoming a one-stop-shop for concerned parents with children lost to the darker recesses of Party Central UK.

'Tell me about her,' I said.

'She's a good person. Kind. Caring. Big hearted, you know. Loads of friends.'

'Let me stop you there.' This is where I would look sympathetic, but over the phone that's difficult. 'Without being insensitive, I need you to imagine she's not your daughter. Can you do that?'

'Ok... why?'

'Now describe her.'

She had my name, sort of: Jo Whiting. They told me she had started at Brighton University, studying nursing, but they found out almost a year into her studies that she had been thrown out after three months. I figured she was one of those students who sees Uni as a paid jaunt.

Apparently when they stopped sending her money they stopped hearing from her. They had tried everything they could, contacting friends, her landlord, even the police, but no one had heard from her, and if she didn't want to be found she wouldn't be. Not by them, anyway. Once their retainer had cleared, an essential part of screening out time-wasters, I got to work.

It was a time consuming one, but I was on expenses so that didn't matter. There were only so many areas of the city where people rented rooms cheaply. There are luxury flats, family flats, and there are student rooms where landlords fleece you because mummy and daddy can afford to pay five-hundred a month for one room of a house. But still in some areas for two-hundred a month you could net yourself a proper shithole. One room of a shithole, mind. People pay in cash and you turf them out if they can't, taking whatever gear they've left behind, which you can sell on the corners or in clubs to make up your losses. A government report came out recently that said Brighton and Hove had some of the least deprived and most deprived areas in the country. One area was so bad it was just outside the bottom one percent, whereas others were some of the most affluent in Britain. The city centre was also fifteenth in the ranking of where in the UK you were most likely to be the victim of a crime.

I could smell drugs in this case. In this town, in this business, you get a nose for it pretty quickly. Until recently Brighton was the drug-death capital of Britain, with more drugs-related deaths per head than any other city. I liked to think that this was because those who were dying were the bastards who came down at the weekend because of its party reputation. They were all fucking Londoners. I hoped. Now the title had been passed to Liverpool, although I'm sure us, London, Cardiff, and Glasgow will be fielding good teams this year.

I spent every day of the week checking more and more hovels. I also checked in with Lenny, a homeless guy whose spot was outside my office.

'Don't recognise her, chief,' he mumbled.

'If I give you the picture could you ask around for a couple of days? Twenty quid in it for you.'

He held out his hand.

'Ten now. Ten when you give me the picture back.'

'What if I find her?'

'Find her and I'll give you fifty.'

It was no good though. The homeless community is pretty well connected, they're always sharing tips about which shelters are good, and which places outside are safe, and yet no one had seen her. That meant she had somewhere to live. Lenny was clean now but he had been on the junk before, so he was able to narrow down my list of places. He had saved me a lot of foot ache and a lot of blisters. That alone was worth the twenty. It was on the Friday that I found her.

It was a house on Upper Lewes Road, one of those ones like Rory's old house, with a split floor where the front is at street level but the back is one story lower. In this case the back of the house was also a scooter repair shop that opened onto the main Lewes Road.

I banged on the front door. No answer. So I picked the lock. I braced myself for confused, strung-out looks. Several times that week I had picked my way into a den only find plenty of people inside. They were simply too high to answer the door. But this time there was no one. Just a rush of air trying to escape. Sick air. I covered my mouth. Drug dens smell of dirt and smoke, this one smelt of death.

I flicked on my torch. At the time I didn't know why it was so dark, but I saw later on that all the windows had been covered in case some nosey neighbour caught them shooting up and decided to call the police.

The place had rats, there were droppings every few steps. I had to kick my way through empty bottles and rotting newspapers as I checked each room. Stained wallpaper. Clusters of dead flies on the windowsills. Dried vomit pools, with chunks in. Strange discarded clothes. Bare, ripped mattresses. In one room a rotted plate of food, forgotten about in a chemical haze. All of these rooms were empty so far, but I could hear something from the one I hadn't checked. A buzzing. It was flies. All the live flies were in one room. Which meant I knew what I was going to find. Only I didn't know exactly what I was going to find.

I pushed open the door and it swung ominously. It stank. I had to bat the flies away from my face. And there she was, a twisted body on the white bedsheet. A few days dead already. Then everyone had scarpered. What junkie wanted to be caught with a dead flatmate, even if it was nothing to do with you.

The sheet, pillow, and some of the wall had been dyed an interesting shade of blood, with just a hint of vomit. It had been painful. I prayed to god she had been too strung-out to feel it.

Something crunched underneath my foot. It was a small clear bag. And inside were two small, round, blue pills. With stars debossed in the centre. I called the police and waited until her dad arrived. I should have pressed him for payment, but I couldn't. I just couldn't.

I came out of my reverie when someone started banging on Rory's door.

'Mr Sweet! Open up!'

I jumped up, unsure what to do. I heard a female voice bark 'Break it down!' and the door smashed into what seemed like a million pieces.

Police officers stormed in and surrounded me, and through the melee I saw the blonde DCI saunter into the room.

She was looking at me. Me standing there with a bloody knife in one hand and a packet of drugs in the other, and she had a wicked smile on her face.

3

Just Another Dead Drug Dealer

UNIFORMS CORRALLED ME to the kitchenette table where the blonde DCI was waiting. I sat down in the chair opposite, doing my best to appear nonchalant. The uniforms closed in around me, blocking any escape. They had the sticky smell of sweat running over "manly" aftershave. Something with a big tattooed sportsman in the advert or a deadly animal on the bottle.

More officers, the younger uniforms, were making phone calls, trying to get in touch with the landlord and not getting very far. Others were moving between floors, asking the neighbours if they had seen or heard anything unusual recently. Mostly they were getting doors slammed in their faces, occasionally with a kind 'fuck off'.

I wondered what they thought I was doing here, in

their position it would certainly give me a lot of thought. I wanted to get up and start doing my job, or get out of here and start doing my job. But I was stuck at the table, just listening, and watching the woman opposite me.

Someone had gone to the effort of making her a cup of tea, and she took her time stirring it, enjoying my captivity, making it plainly clear to me that she was in charge. It may have been my imagination but it seemed as though the splinters from the door were still dancing through the air between us.

Once she had finished stirring and lightly dinged her teaspoon on the side of the cup, she got straight to the point:

'Breaking and entering is a pretty serious charge. But probably the most common for private dickheads.'

So, they thought I had picked my way in, that was interesting. I had the key in my pocket and I could clear my name in seconds. But if I gave them the key I wouldn't get it back, and I might have a reason to visit Rory's place again, so I kept schtum. I could talk my way out of this. And if I couldn't, I had the key anyway.

'Apparently,' she added, 'you have a history of this.'

'Ancient history.'

'Before you started charging for it?'

'Before the pyramids were built. I use my powers for good now.'

She turned her head slightly like a schoolmistress, 'That's the beautiful thing about past convictions: they never go away.'

She was wrong about that, I was never convicted. I had got away with my tail burned and I never looked back.

'This,' she moved on, placing her hand on my flick knife, which was now inside an evidence bag on the table, 'is an illegal weapon.'

She had a much softer voice than before. Nicer, and calmer. Maybe she knew what she was doing.

'It's a tool,' I said.

'A penknife is a tool. A stanley knife is a tool. A butchers knife is a tool. This is a concealed weapon.'

'It wasn't concealed.'

'And what about this morning, on the beach? I don't remember you waving it around then.'

'Maybe I didn't have it on me then.'

She sighed. 'It doesn't matter anyway. It's illegal to carry any kind of flick knife.'

'Good thing it's not mine.'

'Excuse me?'

'I found it here in the flat. I was just using it.'

She narrowed her eyes, she knew that she couldn't prove anything, and on the slim chance that she could it would be a lot of effort for very little. Then again, she might do it just to piss me off.

'Shall we call it a draw?' I asked, 'Or do you want

to go another round?'

She sighed again and passed the knife to one of the officers, who promptly zipped it away in a black bag. At the very least she had got the knife off me, so I had lost something. Then she leaned back in her chair, sipping her tea.

'I've dealt with a hundred guys like you,' she started, 'and I'm not impressed by your toughness. I spend every day with tough guys. What I see very rarely is honesty. That's what impresses me.'

'You have a perfect nose.'

'Excuse me?'

'And wonderful eyes.' She still wasn't impressed. 'Just being honest,' I explained.

'See, you're just the same as the rest.'

'Oh no, I'd say it to any of the guys too, if it were true. But sadly they're ugly as fuck.'

I felt them twitch. They wanted to smack my head into the table.

'I'd love to spend more time with you,' I got up, making sure to push the chair backwards into the officers behind, 'but it puts me off when people are watching.'

One of them tried to block my way, so I grabbed him and pushed him back. Hard. I headed away from the kitchenette, closer to the sofa where there were some younger officers standing by the coffee table. I spoke so that everyone could hear me.

'That body on the beach is a man called Rory Sweet. He was attacked here in his flat. Right where your men are standing.'

I looked at the officers by the coffee table and they froze. From their faces and their glances over my shoulder I could tell that she was subtly gesturing for them to move, which they quickly did. That would teach her.

I heard her whisper 'Get the CSI team in here.' There was a moment of inaction and then 'Now!' People jumped like George had and an officer headed out of the room with that little skip that you put in when you're in a hurry. Everyone started to get to work, or least did a good impression of it.

'He doesn't leave,' she told her men whilst she slipped out to make a phone call.

They stared at me for a few moments, willing me to try and leave so that this time they *could* smack me into the table. Like a pack of three dogs, squared up to me, waiting for the moment when I would look away or turn to run and then they would rip me to shreds. They were salivating as though I was a steak they were about to devour, eyes on every part of me.

'Are you guys trying to steal grooming tips?' I asked. 'I'll give you one, it's called soap.' They smirked, and I swear one of them licked his lips. 'And by grooming, I don't mean that thing you guys do where you pick bits out of each other's hair.'

'You're a funny man, Grabarz,' one of them growled. 'Maybe you should be a comedian. That might pay your bills.'

'Everyone got an email,' another one added, 'the bosses don't want anything to do with you.'

'You were the one guy the force took seriously,' the first one continued, 'so what does that make you now? People want someone to tail their wife, they hire Alderney. They want someone to do some tough guy shit they hire Clyde.'

Perry Clyde, one of the other two detectives in the city, and a big thick lump of meat with veins popping out everywhere like a penis being squeezed in a vice.

'And yet here I am,' I said, 'I know who the victim is, and I'm the one who found the crime scene, and I'm the one your boss is going to look to for answers.'

'She knows what you are, Grabarz.'

'And you, Lurch.'

He took a step towards me, but she returned at the same moment and he stopped where he was, as though he just liked the coffee table more than the others. I milked the moment for everything I could. She gave them a few, uninteresting orders, and then she moved towards me and I pretended to look around.

'So...' she was fishing for information, 'you must have known him pretty well to recognise him like that.'

I kept up the act of studying some obscure vinyl on his record shelf.

'So? How did you do it?' She wasn't giving up, she really wanted to know. In which case, it wasn't something I was going to give away for free.

'I'll tell you. But I want something.'

'No, no. I'm not doing deals.' She seemed disgusted at the idea.

I kept staring at the wall, as though I really didn't mind either way. 'Suit yourself,' I added.

I could almost hear her thinking, she really did want to know. I guess she thought it might be important.

She turned to the officers and spoke with the nicest tone she'd used yet, 'Guys, go have a fag.'

They all gave each other a quick nod and promptly filed out, the younger ones relieved both at the opportunity to have a break, and to get out of this awkward situation. The atmosphere was definitely of something you were better off not knowing about. Meanwhile, the big lumps gave me dirty looks, as though it was somehow them she should be speaking to. I was to be avoided. I was a con artist to them. A time-waster.

'What is it you want?' she asked once we were alone. 'Bearing in mind there's not much I'm willing to give.'

A mug clinked behind her, and she looked around to see one officer still by the kitchen units. He was making himself a cup of tea, of all things. She shot, what I could only imagine were daggers, at him.

'I don't smoke,' he managed feebly.

'Get the fuck out of the here!'

He did that little jump that they were all going to have to get used to and quickly moved to the door. Halfway he realised he was still holding the empty mug and turned back to the kitchenette.

'Just put it down!' she screamed.

He put it down on a chair and mumbled 'sorry' as he ran out the door.

I took this moment to admire her from behind as she huffed and pushed loose strands of her golden hair behind her ears. She looked incredibly fit. Well-trained too, I guessed. Perhaps she had been a tactical officer, or in the Forces somehow. I could see the shape of strong shoulder and back muscles beneath her suit, and I could imagine her toned stomach. Powerful women have always been my weakness, and she was no exception. But she scared me a bit too. She reminded me of a black widow, and I thought that if I ever did get to fuck her she'd probably eat me afterwards.

What did I want from her? What did she really have to offer. I already knew the victim, and how he died would hardly solve who killed him. So the autopsy results would be useless. I could find out about the drugs easily enough, so that was a no. There was only one thing.

'I want the blood work,' I said quietly enough to make clear to her that this was just between us.

'What blood work?' she scowled, something else she didn't know?

'This blood. Here. That's all over the floor. You just can't see it.'

I guess, in her defence, the CSI guys hadn't been in yet, and I hadn't spotted it until it was on my knife. They would spot it in a heartbeat.

I could see her mulling the deal over for a second, but she didn't want to appear weak.

'Fine. So tell me.'

Did she think I was stupid? 'When I get the blood work.'

I made it plainly clear with my eyes that this was the way these things worked. If she really was new to this way of operating, she needed to learn quickly.

'Then fuck off.' Her voice was louder now, and unhappy. 'There won't be any blood work. This murder is second tier now.'

My face must have been a picture. 'Second tier!?' I almost bellowed. What the fuck did that mean?

'Yes, second: as in less important.'

'Is this from you or on high?' I already knew the answer to that. "Second tier" was not the kind of term that would come out of her brain. No, something so couched in bullshit language had to be from up above. If she really was the Chief's special project then it was probably him she had called. Reporting directly to the top. She had updated him on the case and he had determined that this was not the sort of thing that his precious new investment should be dealing with. Either that or murder wasn't a big concern anymore. Not this murder anyway.

'Does it matter?' she replied.

'What exactly makes a *murder* "second tier"?'

'A lot of things.' She changed her footing, ready for any reprisal, 'The likelihood of a result. The public interest. The profile of the victim—'

I cut her off right there and then, 'So *that's* it!' I yelled. I really didn't care at this point if the officers outside could hear me. In fact, I hoped they could. 'Just another dead drug dealer! Who cares!?' And then I really kicked, 'If the killer had been one of your boys they'd've given them a medal.' And I stormed out.

I made it down the stairs without strangling anyone; realising that for a second time I hadn't got her name. That was a standard piece of detective work, I must be off my game. Being around her was like putting a magnet next to a compass. I needed to get away from here, to my office, where I could be alone and just think for a while. Everything had happened so quickly this morning that I had no idea what I made of it yet. And no idea what I was going to do about it.

I came out the back, where I was parked up. The cold winter sun was filtered through thin clouds like a lamp through a veil, over-lighting everything but throwing no shadows. The road was almost completely empty, everyone's cars were at work. Chattering, screeching seagulls shouted to each other from the rooftops. The sound of someone drilling in a road far away bounced off the walls of houses. A train rolled over the bridge, moving between London Road and Moulsecoomb stations, and then out of here towards Lewes and Eastbourne. That would be nice.

Here was the police van, open at the back, with the large packet of pills split open, and all the small bags lying around. The big lumps were surrounding it and when they saw me they all shoved their hands in their pockets. They might as well have started whistling for how convincing the act was. I didn't know if they were planning to take them personally, sell them back to the dealers, or to new customers and run a racket themselves. Whichever way, my faith in the police of this town sank one notch lower, if that was even possible. I think I must have muttered 'Jesus Christ', and just kept walking.

4

Everyone Has to Pay Rent

I RODE DOWN from Rory's place back toward my office. One of the good things about Brighton is that if you have a car or a motorbike almost everything is within five or ten minutes reach. I kept a couple of rooms above Lambton's jewellers in the Lanes. I liked being there as it was both easy for clients to find and easy for me to disappear amongst the network of interconnected pedestrian alleys that is perhaps the city's best feature. Superior to either the Pier or the Pavilion, they conjure up Brighton's past far more vividly than a tourists' promenade or a royal summer house ever could. The Lanes were part of the Old Town and were where the real people had lived. You can see this history on a map, where the Lanes are bordered by North Street, East Street, West Street, and the sea, and cut down the middle by Middle Street.

Like all pieces of history they get their fair share of tourists. In Meeting House Lane they used to faint with horror at the bricked up cell where the Grey Nun was buried alive. The story went that she had eloped with a soldier. Silly nun, you might think, but even sillier tourists: walk a few steps further down the lane and it's obvious the "bricked-up cell" is actually a bricked up doorway in the garden wall of the Quaker meeting house. Which is not the same meeting house that gives the Lane its name, by the way, even if people tell you it is.

The cottages that make up most of the Lanes were of course built for the fishermen, seeing as that was the industry the town was pretty-much founded on. Now they consist mostly of jewellers and cafés, with the odd pub, restaurant, or some specialist shop thrown in, and that's why the tourists flock there now.

A shopping district it may be, but in every cellar and hidden hole you can feel the influence of Brighton's smugglers, which in many ways had been a bigger industry than fishing ever was. The real place the tourists should flock to is Black Lion Lane where hidden down a twitten barely wide enough for one person are the oldest surviving buildings of the Old Town. Although not as old as some people claim. Estate agents especially. I had my eye on one, it would be great to live in a piece of history. Especially one so close to the office.

I parked in my lock-up and headed into a café. I couldn't really afford breakfast at the moment but the place round the corner had accepted credit from me in the past. It was very-Brighton: avocado toast, with a pickled-radish slaw. Soda bread, of course, normal bread just won't do. I really wished the greasy spoon would accept credit, but I guess they weren't that naive. And I suppose I was coming around to avocado toast. A man with a moustache wider than his head made me a really fantastic coffee, which I'll admit is something hipsters are so much better at, and after I had used it to wash down the breakfast, I wandered toward the office.

Rory was dead. What did that mean for me? It felt like it should mean everything, but I hadn't seen him in years. Eight, nine, even ten perhaps. Is it possible to be that good a friend and not see someone for a third of your life? Was I just kidding myself?

No. No I wasn't. Rory had done so much for me when we were young. If we hadn't seen each other it was because I was a lousy friend. I was too proud. But then what about starz?

He was selling starz. So maybe he didn't deserve my sympathy at all. I had seen what they could do, first hand. They killed people. If you knew they killed people, and you still sold them then you were as good as a murderer in my book. That's what I had told myself the last few months. My brain told me that nothing had changed just because Rory turned out to be one of them. Fuck him. It just felt different.

All these thoughts and more were swirling through my mind as I passed the little alcove where Lenny often makes his camp. He was there again, in his trademark ushanka and Army Surplus coat. It was because of that combination that people nicknamed him Lenin when he first appeared on the streets, despite him being from Liverpool and not Saint Petersburg. Later it got shortened to Lenny and he went by it now. His real name was John.

'Morning, Lenny, how are you doing?' I asked as I moved past him.

'Alright, you know, boss. Alright.'

He was smiling, I took that as an omen that today might, after all, get better not worse.

'How has this morning been?' I realised I needed to have a conversation that wasn't about a dead friend.

'Damp.'

'What do you do if it's damp?'

'Move around. Nothing much more you can do.'

'Where have you been?'

By this point I was squatting down next to him, leaning on the wall, getting some strange looks from the tourists and shoppers walking past who were wondering why I had broken the rules and actually spoken to someone on the street.

'Job Centre.'

'Any luck?'

'They made me wait around for ages. But they always do that.'

'No hope of actually getting a job then?'

'No fixed address, chief. No one wants to know.'

'That's tough. No luck getting a place?'

'In this city?'

'Good point.' I couldn't argue with that, I was practically on the sharp end of it myself. 'What made you come to Brighton?'

'I spent two days living in Gatwick. I had enough for a coach, the first coach I saw was coming here.'

'Why were you living in the airport?'

'I was in America.'

'America? You never told me that.'

'Yeah. Twenty-five years. New York and San Francisco.'

'Doing what?'

'Construction, you know. Manual stuff.'

'Did you like it?'

'Yeah, but it's a bad place to be out of work.'

'What do you mean by that?'

'Just what it sounds like. Did you know, in New York the bars are just for Italians, Irish, black fellas, etc.?'

'No, I didn't.'

I liked it when he told me stories. I guess because they were honest. No bullshit, just what he had seen.

'I knew some black fellas, and you see they all hated me because they thought I was Irish. Irish-American. People would say, "no, he's English" and they would go "Oh, England, we like it there." One fella said "I went to London, and there were black folks and white folks in the same bars." I said, "What do you mean?", he said, "Here, we have to look in through the windows, and if there's no black folks inside we can't go in." Terrible.'

'That is terrible.'

He had successfully diverted my attention, I was having thoughts about something else for the first time today.

'Brighton is the best place to be homeless,' he continued.

'Why's that?'

'Have you ever been anywhere else, London, Liverpool, Manchester, and seen someone walking down the street, singing to themselves?'

'Not that I can remember. Why?' I wasn't sure what this had to do with homelessness.

'People look at them, point at them and stuff. Shout things at them. In Brighton, that doesn't happen because people can just be who they want to be. It's like two men or two women kissing, everywhere else people take a second look, they tut or something. But here they don't. And it goes the same for us folks, I get my share of looks but as long as it's looks and not people shouting I'm alright.'

'I guess I take it for granted,' I said, 'not having lived anywhere else.'

'You shouldn't.'

I smiled and patted him on the shoulder. 'Nice chatting with you, Lenny.' I stood up. 'What you up to the rest of the day?'

'Go to the library. Spend most of the day in there when it's cold.'

'What do you do to pass the time, do you read?'

'Watch movies on my phone. Free Wi-Fi in there.'

I still found it funny that these days even guys without somewhere to live have a smartphone. That says a lot, doesn't it? Which problems we fix. Rather than give people homes, we've given them a power socket and Wi-Fi, and the best they can do is escape to a world of pirated films.

'There's some nice pair of shoes waiting for you up there.' This was Lenny's way of saying someone had gone in the street door to my office and not come out.

'Heels or brogues?'

'Slip-ons. But a man.'

'Thanks.'

I stood up to more strange looks and took the few short steps down Meeting House Lane.

I left the street door unlocked during the day, that way people could let themselves in and wait on the landing. So far this had not been abused, even by

Lenny, who could just sit inside the door to get away from the cold, but didn't. I was pretty sure that in his position I wouldn't be so honourable.

I made it up the stairs to the tiny landing outside my office, the boards creaking beneath my feet. Some-one was indeed waiting on one of the beaten-up wooden chairs outside my beaten-up wooden door. From behind I could see them reading the words etched on the rippled glass window: "J. GRABARZ" and underneath, "No.1 Private Detective". A client, at last. I needed a paying job. I rounded the corner and took a look at him.

He was too smart. Thirty-odd with a tailored three-piece suit and slip-on leather shoes with silly tas-sels. The hair on the top of his head was a shiny slicked black liquorice and the bottom half was designer stub-ble. I got the distinct feeling that he went to the gym, and had a skincare routine. Not a client.

I got out my key and slipped it into the lock.

'Mr Grabarz?' he intoned. Anyone who intones my name normally wants a piece of me.

'I'm his cleaner.'

'Rufus Grimace.'

He said it like it should mean something to me. I suppose it did, but I resented that.

'Lawyer.' I spat the word at him like an insult, which it was, and left my key hanging in the door.

'You hate lawyers, I'm sure.'

'I love lawyers.' I smiled as genuinely as I could pretend, 'Estate Agents. Politicians. Anyone who makes me feel like I have scruples.'

He ignored the joke, 'You haven't replied to any of our letters.'

I had been getting two a week from his firm for the last month, but lots of people have tried to demand money from me, and they never get it.

'Your client didn't like what I found,' I said, 'so he refused to pay. I can live with that, it's part of the job. But threatening to sue me, just to get their retainer back? That's low.'

'No one is threatening to sue you.' Now it was his turn to grin, 'They *are* suing you.'

He pushed an envelope into my chest so that I had no choice but to take it. A court summons, no doubt. I saw a flash of silver from his inside pocket as he did it.

I took a longer look at his tailored suit, pampered face, and oily hair before I spoke. The suit had a not-too-subtle plaid pattern, and with it a flashy melton, second right pocket, and contrast stitching. Every extra option a tailor gives you. When people with no taste get their first bespoke suit, they always go too far. This specimen had obviously ascended into high-end people-milking and transferred the money from his first payslip straight to Gresham Blake.

'Your retainer clearly costs more than mine, what

exactly do they expect to get out of me?' I asked.

He chuckled, 'Well, not money.'

'What does that mean?' I asked through gritted teeth.

'There are other private detectives in this city.'

'Yeah: two. Who was it, Alderney or Clyde?'

'We know exactly how many pounds are in your bank balance, Mr Grabarz. And it's not even enough to cover this month's rent, is it. Let alone last month's too.'

I wanted to punch him, but I resisted the urge and reserved my anger for Clarence Alderney. Clarence was the respectable private dick in this town. The one the rich went to. He was second-generation Sri Lankan Tamil and counter-programmed this by dressing like a Raj colonialist. He always wore a cream suit and carried an ivory-topped cane, despite being hardly older than me. He was a good detective for those kinds of small cases. The no-danger kind. I was surprised he was willing to work against another private eye though. It felt to me like he was breaking some kind of code. But as I knew too well, everyone has to pay rent.

I acted like it was nothing, 'So it's Alderney then. Clyde can't count.'

I'd like to think he bought it, but he was smarter than that. He just turned to leave. Perhaps he was embarrassed for me. How dare he be embarrassed for me?

'Wait,' I said.

He turned back, trying to keep the pity out of his face.

I stepped forward and reached a hand underneath his jacket, into his inside pocket, he barely flinched. Pulling out his silver business card holder, I popped it open, slid a card into my hand, clipped it back shut, and gently put it back in his pocket.

'How else will I get in touch?' I explained, uncomfortably close to him.

He turned to leave again, but after a few steps he stopped.

'My client doesn't want your money, Mr Grabarz,' he said with a smirk on the back of his head, 'Just your reputation.'

He started down the stairs.

'Is that all?' I called.

'That or you can do the job you were hired to do: investigate ABC Construction.'

And with that, he was gone.

I remembered that. *Investigate ABC Construction*, it was all I had been told. It had been a phone call, a week after the police blacklisted me. I was feeling miserable and probably in a stupor. The rain lashing against my office window, and I could hear two cats screaming at each other over the last dry spot in the alley. I was drinking beer again. The problem with me and beer is that I can drink it like water.

The phone rang and a male voice told me that they would pay five-thousand pounds for me to 'investigate ABC Construction'.

'That's all you want to tell me?' I had asked.

'Your client is very cautious, Mr Grabarz.'

'Really, well if *you're* not my client, who is?'

'Your client is the person who's paying you.'

'Listen, mate, I'm very cautious too.'

There was the sound of some thinking from the other end of the line.

'I might be working for a criminal,' I added.

'Would that be a problem?'

'Not necessarily. But I'd rather know before I did the job than find out afterwards when the police break down my door.' At least if they told me no I could say they told me no.

'There's no need to worry, Mr Grabarz. It's nothing like that.'

The client was Todman Concrete, he said. It wasn't a front as far as I knew. Looking back now, the voice could have been Grimace, the lawyer. I insisted on a fifteen-percent retainer. I used to get thirty.

I figured Todman had more money than sense and wanted to do due diligence on ABC before they gave them any contracts, or something like that. Maybe I saw it as a way of making a good amount of money for very little work. Maybe.

I read in the Argus that ABC Construction and Todman Concrete had had a ruckus, and that it was slowing the building of the new development down in the marina. I doorstepped their press agent one wet morning.

'Mr Singh?'

'Yes, who are you?'

To tell him, I had to chase the silver-haired man as he hurried to his BMW: 'Dan Harman, from The Argus,' I handed him a business card that said just that.

'What do you want?'

'I'm writing a story about this ruckus with Todman Concrete. Care to comment?'

He sighed, 'Sadly they did not meet the high standards we expected from their firm.'

He went to open his car door but I stood where it would open so that he had to deal with me first.

'What does that mean? That could mean almost anything.'

'If you don't mind, I want to get out of this rain. Make an appointment at our office.'

'I can't do that, I'm spending the rest of the day with Todman, they're very happy to talk.'

'I'm sure they are.' He sighed again. 'Look, we needed a higher grade mix of concrete than they supplied. The whole building could have come down.

And if you don't know what that means, go to the library and look it up.'

I stepped out of the way of his door.

'Now if you don't mind, I'm getting wet.'

Nothing too unusual in that. So I went to my usual sources, I didn't have any in the building trade. Lenny hadn't heard anything fishy through the grapevine and neither had George.

'They're clean, Joe. I know it.'

'I'm giving you fifty quid so just run them through the system for me.'

'There's no need,' he insisted.

'I'm giving you fifty quid.'

He ran them, and he was right, they came up clean. There was nothing dodgy with ABC as far as the police were concerned.

With that done, I needed my five grand so I wired them what I had found and waited for the money to turn up in my account. That's when the letters started.

I had done a "poor job", and they demanded their retainer back. This happens a lot in the trade. People hire you to find proof of something, and when it turns out to be untrue they refuse to pay. Textbook denial. They're convinced you didn't look hard enough. They threaten you and sometimes harass you, but they eventually leave you alone. Especially if you give them a smack round the head. But Todman Concrete were one of the biggest firms in the South East, they could afford to sue me just out of spite. They wanted my reputation? The police had stripped that from me already.

Another man passed Grimace on the stairs as he left and jogged up to the landing. He looked around my age, but everything about him said middle class, comfortable living. He was wearing a polo-neck with some kind of symbol over the left breast. What symbol doesn't matter, just the presence of a logo seems to say "I can afford to buy nice things, unlike you", although a lot of the time it just says "I have more money than sense." On top he wore a jacket, also branded, but this time the sort of brand designed to get you to the top of Everest. And jeans, with a satchel at his side. He looked clean shaven and well-rested, two things I have never managed to achieve. Sometimes I get one, but never both.

I watched him read the words on my door, then he held out a hand for me to shake.

'Joe Grabarz?'

'Yes.' I didn't shake it.

'My name's Jordan Murrows, I'm a reporter.'

He handed me a card. It just had his name, a phone number, and an email address. No logo.

'From the Argus?'

'Freelance.'

He got out a recording device and turned it on. It

was in my face.

'You must be new, Jordan.'

'I am. I just moved here from London.'

He had that restless energy about him that good reporters often have. Bad reporters can have it too though.

'Really?' I said, 'Wanted to get out of the big smoke?'

'Yeah, get some of the sea air. Brighton's a much nicer town, I think.'

I nodded, 'You're the reason people born and raised here can't buy houses.'

He didn't really have a reply for that. He'd soon develop one. But he must be tougher than he looked, he had already spent several years being told to fuck off on a daily basis.

'Apparently you're some kind of detective.'

Now it was my turn to read the words on my door. What a clever man. 'That's right.'

'You were on the beach this morning where the body was found.'

'What body?'

'I have photos.' He smiled. The bastard, he had long-lensed me. He knew how to put a man in a corner. 'With these kind of grisly details those photos are going to be front page tomorrow. May even make the evening editions today. And online. Care to comment about what you were doing there?'

'On the record?' I asked.

'Absolutely.'

I leaned into the microphone. 'I was fisting your sister.'

He sighed and stopped the recording.

'Now fuck off,' I added. And he did.

Once he had finished slamming the downstairs door on his way out, I took the court summons from my pocket. There was something else in there. That photo of Rory and Thalia.

Thalia. If I could find her that quickly others would be right behind me. The police would definitely want to speak to her. But there might be others, those who Rory was mixed up with, who could think for some foolish reason that she might know something. As though she would be stupid enough to be involved. Still, the thought concerned me, so I slipped the envelope under my door and headed back down the stairs.

5

The Little Sister

I CALLED ON the dry-cleaners and found that Thalia had gone home. 'Personal reasons', I was disapprovingly told. That meant she already knew, someone had called her. Police, maybe. Seemed unlikely. More likely they had called on Elaine and she had called Thalia. Either way, I extracted her address from the owners and headed on my way.

It was off The Avenue in Bevendean, the sort of place she could just about afford. A one-bedroom ground-floor flat, apparently, but again being Brighton, "ground floor" could mean a basement or first floor if the ground isn't flat. The place was round the corner from a commercial strip of takeaways, corner shops, and bookies. No trendy independent coffee shops here. Bevendean has a reputation as the best of the three worst areas of Brighton. It goes Bevendean,

Moulsecoomb, Whitehawk. Don't go there.

But as I rode up The Avenue, which orbits a large grassy strip that splits lower Bevendean in two, I was struck by quite how much green there was here in this "awful" part of Brighton. I could imagine that in summer, with the sun shining, these green spaces would be filled with children playing football and dogs leaping around madly.

So why was this considered such a bad place? In the little time I had to think about it I could only come up with two reasons. The first was aesthetic. It wasn't exactly a beautiful place. Twentieth century social housing, or thereabouts, all brick boxes with no interesting features. No history here, in Bevendean. And the transmitter tower looming above everyone at the top of the hill didn't exactly give the place a relaxing atmosphere.

The second reason was perhaps the most obvious: because this is where poor people live. And if poor people live somewhere then it must be terrible. But with the same money, and given a choice between a bungalow in Bevendean and a cramped Hove or seafront flat I think I know which I would choose. Not that anyone was giving me that choice.

That had to be it: Bevendean was a bad area because poor people lived here. Poor people like Thalia. And like me.

Maybe I was being a bit too sentimental about the

place. The speed bumps I was weaving past told me this was the kind of place where the sound of mopeds wakes you up throughout the night.

I parked up at the end of the road, and strolled in the right direction. The roads were eerily quiet. Maybe it was the weather. There was still an uncomfortable mist lingering in the air, giving everything an unnatural sheen. A pearlesence.

I was looking for number seventeen and counted the odd numbers on the odd houses with their cracked rendering as I passed them. Seven, nine, eleven... I could already see where seventeen was: the door was open and I could hear someone shouting. I broke into a jog, then marched up the two-or-three steps to the open door, ready for anything.

There was Thalia, in the hallway. A very tall, broad man my age had his big hands around her little throat.

'Where is it!?' he was shouting.

Another man my age, shorter, skinnier, and hairy all over, was leaning against the wall, watching with frisky yellow eyes. He looked insultingly relaxed with what was happening. It was him who noticed me, standing up off the wall and blocking my path.

'This is none of your business, mate.'

He had a pointy face, and was gangly, which in tandem with his wiry body hair that seemed to tie itself in knots around his wrists, gave him the odd persona of a weasel. He was no real threat.

I pushed him into the wall. Hard. Something smashed, and he crumpled to the floor. The big man was too slow to react, only just having time to release his grip on Thalia before I kicked him in the stomach. It sent him backwards through the kitchen door and out of sight. It was a saloon door, and it definitely needed oiling as it swung back and forth on its hinges.

She had just a second to regain her breath, 'Thanks—' but before she could finish he was back up.

I grabbed her by the arm and threw her into the next room. Luckily she landed in an arm chair. I would later claim this was deliberate.

He squared up. Angered, he seemed to have swelled to an even bigger size, filling the entire hall-way. Everything about him was double sized, even his features.

Sweat ran down his back. Adrenaline shot through my veins. He snorted and huffed, his hot breath condensing in the cold air, looking for all the world like a shaved bear.

He jabbed. I jumped backwards, dodging it. He jabbed again. I jumped backwards again. I was going to fall out the door at this rate. He jabbed a third time and followed it with a right hook. I deflected it and used his enormous momentum to send him sailing past me towards the door, but he stopped just short.

The thin man climbed back up and tried to take a swing at me. It was so poorly thrown that I just leant backwards and took the time to slip my hand into my pocket, into my trusty brass knuckles. When I came back at him my fist connected right in the middle of his face. His nose shattered, and he fell backwards, past the big man, out the door and down the front steps.

The bear then jabbed again, I deflected as I had before, but I hadn't seen him pull a belt knife. Deflecting that cut my hand up pretty badly.

Now all the rules had gone, which is the way I like to fight. So I kicked him as hard as I could in the groin. He dropped the knife and dropped to his knees. I gave him a helping shove and he rolled out the door and down the front steps. His friend half caught him. Clutching him whilst he clutched his broken nose.

There they lay, the bear and the weasel. And as I looked down on them, I thought that I recognised them. I had almost realised who they were when the thought was interrupted.

'Do you know who we work for!?' the weasel spat.

'Don't talk,' I barked, 'Run.'

They picked themselves up and took about a second too long doing it, so I marched one step towards them. They left. Quickly.

Once they had rounded the corner I headed back into the house to find Thalia brushing herself down. I got up close. Perhaps too close. Perhaps just the right amount of close. And checked her neck for marks. It was a lovely neck. She would be all right. She smiled at me, nervous. I was very close. I nodded and turned to leave but she grabbed my arm. Suddenly I realised that my hand had been hurting badly for the last minute or so.

We sat, and as she bandaged me up we spoke very little.

'I remember,' she started, 'when you and Rory pulled Laurie Norman and Amy Rattley off me, it was the only time I'd seen you be the tough ones.'

'That was Rory. I just helped.'

'What were the names of those three boys who bullied you?'

'I don't remember,' I lied.

That was all we said. I spent the rest of the time glancing around the room. The place was filled with what I assumed was other people's old furniture, donated or bought cheap online. She had done her best to make a virtue of it. Shabby-chic, upcycling, and all those things where people ruin great craftsmanship and for some reason it increases the value. Despite her efforts it was clear she was struggling. After all, she was living in Brighton on minimum wage.

As I listened to the sound of her neighbours screaming the place down through the walls, I decided she wasn't safe here, and there was only one place that would do.

* * *

I had to stop into my office first so we headed down that way. She held on tight to me as she rode pillion, her ample assets pressed against my back. I enjoyed giving her a couple of shakes and scares over speed bumps and round chicanes. When we made it to the Lanes I parked up and led her toward the office. Lenny had already left for the library.

With my bandaged hand I pushed open the door with my name on it, 'I just need to grab something,' and headed into my office at the back.

Thalia waited in the outer office where clients are supposed to be received, taking a look around. It was quite dark, with it being an overcast winter day and the only windows being in my office. There was a desk covered in a dirty sheet, a pot plant quietly dying in the corner, and little else.

The floor was bare wood, unvarnished, and scuff-marked. The walls could do with more than a lick of paint. More like a big wet snog of paint. And I've never been very good at dusting. Kids would've had a great time drawing pictures in it. Also, if there was a world prize for the best collection of dead flies, I would have won hands down. I had a great big one as the centre-piece exhibit.

I could hear her stepping on the court summons and placing it on top of the covered desk.

'Are you decorating?' she called.

'I decided to stop pretending my secretary was running errands. Plus...' I sighed, dropping one piece of armour, 'business has been a little slow the last few months. Since the police blacklisted me.'

'You can't have relied on them for all your jobs?'

'No, but I did rely on them for my reputation. I like to be able to pick my clients.'

'But now you take whoever?'

I found what I was looking for, a small kit case in my bottom drawer, and came back out to join her.

'Only when I really have to eat.'

The short winter day was turning to evening by the time we made it to my place. We walked along the Old Steine and up London Road to Preston Circus. It's only a short walk and I still haven't been able to find a cheap lock-up nearby.

My flat is the only one I could find in my price range anywhere near the office. It sits almost within the shadow of the viaduct, opposite the Duke of York's cinema, next to a pub, and two stories above a hearing aid shop.

We trudged up the stairs, stress-tiredness catching up with both of us, and after my key made a good fist of not letting me in, I showed her over the threshold.

'This is it.'

It was the first time, probably in a couple of years

that I had let anyone into my flat. Not that you need to feel sorry for me, I just like my own space. But seeing it through someone else's eyes for once made me see it unbiased. It was a dump. A one-bedroom place with no bed. Just a mattress on the floor. In the other room there was a sofa, a few kitchen units, and a television. Everything was dirty.

'It's… lovely.'

Thalia was kind, but she still did that awkward dance people do when they're not sure where is safest to sit down.

We ordered a couple of pizzas, but we both ate less than half. We were physically hungry, but too caught up in our own thoughts to put the effort into actually eating. Once they were cold I put them in the fridge so that I could have a breakfast without debt for once.

I relaxed her with a drink, I had some Tuaca in the freezer, and she stood and stared out the one window.

I always thought that view was a great microcosm of modern Brighton. The arthouse cinema, the independent coffee shop, the permit-only parking spaces squeezed tightly against the side of the road. The once-noble four-storey buildings carved up into pokey flats. The bicycles chained to railings. The franchise corner shop complete with owner out front, nonchalantly smoking a spliff.

Thalia lit a cigarette. I was worried this would make her look too much like her mother for my liking, but rather than the thick, branded ones her mum smoked, she had rolled some minutely thin ones that gave off nothing but tiny wisps of smoke that disappeared into nothing soon enough. No doubt she was trying to quit.

I felt like I had seen her for the first time today. It was as though someone had cleared the cache of small memories you keep that make up your knowledge of a person. Maybe I had erased them myself, deciding they weren't important. Just Rory's little sister. Now I had to create a new impression from what I saw in front of me.

She really was unlike her mother in every way. Curvy, rather than stick thin. Long dark hair, rather than a dyed bob. And wearing her troubles heavily on her shoulders, rather than carefree. Then again, Elaine was wearing her troubles all over her face these days.

I felt sorry for Thalia, as much as I'm capable. She needed to smile more. But what was there for her to smile about?

I was sitting at my little work table. For a guilty moment I imagined her thick, strong legs wrapped around me, and I decided to concentrate harder on using the kit from my office to clean and disinfect my, bloody, knuckleduster.

As her cigarette burnt down to the last millimetres of rizla, she spoke out of nowhere.

'You know, I asked him about you recently.'

'You saw him?' I realised that was stupid after I said

it. After all, she had a key to his flat.

'Every couple of weeks we would meet up for coffee.'

'Coffee? The last time I saw him he didn't drink anything other than Red Stripe. Probably washed in the stuff too.'

'When was that?'

When *was* that? Could it be as long as ten years ago? We had already started to drift apart even before we turned twenty. I liked to think it was because he turned to crime, but really it was because we turned to different crimes. He had started selling weed, getting in with some pretty shady people. And selling something actually harmful to people in the process.

I, meanwhile, was busy "housebreaking" as it was known. A victimless crime in my mind, if people were smart enough to have contents insurance. Ten, twelve, fifteen years ago when DVD players and stereo systems were still expensive and worth buying and selling on the sly. I would follow people, study their routine, and wait until I knew they were away. Then I would pick my way in, old style, and half-inch everything I could carry. I would sell it to Big Dave down in Whitehawk, and soon I was becoming one of his regulars. It got to the point where sometimes Big Dave would send a kid with me so I could pass him out a load and keep at it. Thankfully for me, someone rescued me and turned me into a private detective of all things.

I thought I could do the same thing for Rory. "Grabarz & Sweet," it had a nice ring to it. Rory had all the same skills I had, pretty much, and the different ones were complimentary. We could be a hell of a good team. It would be like the fantasies we had played at school, but for real.

I arranged to go for a drink with him, expecting to have my old mate back, but he was already gone. I remember sitting in The Signalman, with butterflies in my stomach like it was a blind date. It might as well have been.

A man entered, smiled at me, slapped me on the shoulder, and said "ello, Joe,' and I had absolutely no idea who he was. I honestly didn't know. Five seconds later, when he asked me what I wanted to drink, I realised he must be Rory. It was terrifying. My brain didn't recognise the man who had been my best and only friend since as long as I could remember. Maybe there was a reason why.

The man who sat in front of me and sank drink after drink was some deluded loser who really thought that drug taking and drug dealing was the route to wealth and happiness, and not a cancer that slowly eats down to your bones. I didn't even try to argue with him, this Rory might beat the shit out of me if I did.

I tried to walk him home, genuinely fearing for his life, he might choke if he passed out. It was just my luck that he lived in Moulsecoomb.

I listened to his bullshit all the way down Lewes Road until it really becomes the A270 and leaves Brighton. In the dirty underpass opposite the bottom of Coldean Lane he started to throw up and collapsed.

I stared dead-eyed under the flickering urine-coloured strip lights, inhaling the stench of actual urine, watching Rory's wild hair fluttering as he struggled and slipped in a pool of his own vomit. I felt such contempt for him. It was as though someone else had taken the Rory that I loved, the best man I had known, and destroyed him. He faded into unconsciousness. I just walked away.

'Years ago,' was how I answered Thalia. 'On top of swimming in beer he had just started selling weed.'

She sat down and began sinking into the sofa.

'He started selling because he couldn't afford the amount he was buying. That's when you dropped out.'

'I didn't drop out,' I almost snapped.

'Fine, drifted away.'

Fair enough.

She continued, 'It got to the point where I would never see him. Just a text on my birthday. Christmas if I was lucky.' She sighed, even she was disappointed, 'Then he started taking coke. So he started selling that.'

'He was always a pushover.'

I had finished cleaning my knuckleduster and put

it away.

'But then he got clean!' She said it with a smile.

'When?' I turned to properly look at her, back in detective mode.

'A few months ago.'

'That's when you started seeing him again?'

'Yeah. He finally wised up!' She was smiling somewhat unconvincingly, as though she wanted me to believe it because if I believed it, maybe she could to.

'Maybe,' I offered.

She didn't like that, frowning at me and flaring her nostrils. This was a sore subject already.

'You were always too hard on him.'

'He still dealt, Thalia.'

'No he didn't! He was finished!' She shouted it like I had been saying it a thousand times.

I had pocketed a bag of starz at his flat. I threw them down on the table.

'They call it a legal high,' I wasn't hiding my anger now, 'but I've seen what these things can do.'

She didn't look at them, instead she looked disappointed at *me* now.

'So, what?' She slammed her drink down. 'Now you don't care? I can't pay you. Mum definitely can't.' I knew what they thought of me.

'He was my friend—'

'Didn't you live with us for a bit!?'

'Just for a couple of years.' It was true.

She was holding back tears. I wasn't trying to upset her, so I calmed down.

'You said you asked him about me. Why would you do that?'

'I thought you were a good influence,' she mumbled.

I almost laughed. I've been accused of a lot of things in my time, but never that. 'What did he say?'

'He said if I was ever in trouble, go find you.'

That hurt more than anything.

6

The Bastard Behind It All

I STOOD WITH THALIA, over the mattress.

'You can sleep in the bed.'

'Oh, ok. Where are you going to sleep?' she asked.

'In the bed.'

'Oh… ok.' She didn't move, 'I'm not some little girl with a crush anymore, Joe.'

'I know.' Believe me, I knew.

We lay in bed, together, but separate. I think we were both awake for the two hours that passed, listening to the sounds of the city. The window in the bedroom looks out onto flat roofs, and is inside a small square that all the other flats look into. It was what I imagined a New York tenement building was like. You could hear everything. And I mean everything. In this case a couple I worried about who did nothing but argue and fuck. This evening it was fucking, and there's nothing more awkward than lying next to someone in bed whilst you can hear other people fucking. Why aren't *we* doing that? That's what you're thinking. But you can't do that, because then you'd have to admit the sounds were turning you on. No, you just have to lay there and listen, pitching a tent in the process.

From the other window, the one in the living room, we could hear the far more sanitary sounds of the city at night. Drunk people. Sirens. Taxis idling. But we ourselves were completely silent. That's until I heard a quiet mewing. I could feel the moisture in the air. Thalia was crying. She was trying to hold it in, but soon she was sobbing and sniffling. I know I should have comforted her, but I was busy grappling with my own emotions, and I didn't even know what they were yet. So I got up.

I stepped out of my door, into the circus. The cloud had cleared from the sky and it seemed that there was nothing but distance separating me from the stars. The wind whipped in. It was coming in over the sea, and I could taste the salt. Whenever I left Brighton on my bike, heading north to Ditchling or wherever, when I came back over the Downs and the cold sea air caught me on my neck I knew I was home.

I wandered down London road. There are no clubs and it was past pub closing time so the only lights on were from the various late-night kebab joints, and the only people those staring vacantly from behind the counters. By day, London Road is slowly becoming more gentrified, filling with independent coffee-houses and delis, but by night it is still the same old shithole it always was.

I made it past the Old Steine, where there was more life; zombies dribbling from the centre, trudging their way home to the suburbs. Then I made it into the now pitch-black twittens of the Lanes, and there was only one man around.

Lenny. He looked half frozen, despite his hat. I was sure he would die if he stayed there tonight.

'Why aren't you at the shelter, Lenny!?'

It was insanely cold, especially now that I had stopped moving.

'No beds.'

'Seriously?'

'Plus they don't let you in if you've been drinking.'

'Chrissakes, Lenny! There's a storm coming.'

'Storm Joseph.'

'What?'

'Storm Joseph. That's what the Met Office named it.'

'Well, Storm Joseph is going to kill you if you don't get inside.'

'Where?'

That was a good question. There was only one

good answer.

'Fine. You can sleep on my stairs.'

'Are you sure?'

'I'm sure. At the bottom though, I don't want you making a habit of it.'

It sounds harsh, but technically they're not mine, they're not part of the lease.

I unlocked the outside door and let us both into the warm. Well, not into the warm, but at least out of the cold. Lenny started to set up camp just inside the door, there's not even a square-metre there, it really was pitiful.

'Come on, Lenny, you can sleep on the landing.'

'No, no, chief. Here's just fine.'

I sighed. 'The door's on the latch if you need to go out for a piss. Just don't let it shut behind you or you'll be stuck out there.'

'Thanks, boss.'

'I'd ask you up for a drink but you've had enough.'

Once up into my office I tried to coax the boiler into life, it would be even worse if Lenny died after I'd let him in. Then it really would be my fault.

I didn't bother to turn on the lights, the yellow street lamps and the blue moonlight filtered through the blinds was enough.

For the first time, I spotted quite how dead the pot plant was. I touched a leaf and it came off in my hand, turning to mulch. There was a stale bottle of water on the floor from god-knows-when. I poured it into the soil.

The evening edition had been left outside my door, I picked up it and the unopened court summons as I passed the unused desk, taking both into my back office.

The headline was "GRUESOME BODY FOUND ON BEACH" and the article was by new-boy Jordan. It was fairly good, except it played down the drug angle, no one cared about a dead drug dealer, but if he could be anyone then they cared. It could be them. There was no mention of me anywhere in it, and I was only a silhouette in the photos.

I leant back into my chair. My office was supposed to look reassuring. When I started the business I furnished everything as best I could, doing all the work myself. I could imagine rich older women with cigarettes in cigarette holders sitting opposite me as I leant forward to light them. My secretary would show them in, take all the calls, and perhaps be my little bit on the side. But things hadn't gone that way. Instead I had to work every hour I had just to scrape a living. And a combination of having no time and no one to look after the office meant that nothing was fixed, repaired, or repainted. Sure, I had worked a few times with the police, which is a real validation for a shamus, and meant that I felt I was actually doing something useful, but that was over now too. This office was all I really had, and if I couldn't pay the rent I wouldn't have that soon either.

I needed to stop feeling sorry for myself so I picked up the phone on my desk and dialled the one true friend I had made at the force.

Andy Watson has always been fascinated by criminal systems. The organisation behind organised crime. A few years ago he took it on himself to begin mapping local crime connections. First as a web, and later as a pyramid: we soon discovered that there had always been one man at the top.

Because of his undying devotion to good work he had long been banished to a basement office. But despite being shunned by his superiors, Andy is perpetually relaxed. He once told me he prefers the basement: he's left to do what he's good at, and people always come knocking eventually.

When you look at him he could be a surfer dude or a hippy, with his beard and his top-knot, but instead he's the best crime analyst I've ever met. Sure, it was late, but he was a workaholic.

It rang for some time, and for a moment I thought he was either still out or actually asleep for once.

'Hello?' His voice always had a smile in it, no matter the time, no matter the circumstances.

'Hi, Andy.'

'Trust you to be calling me so late.'

Maybe the smile faded just a bit when he knew it

was me. Just a bit though, that was all he could manage. I could hear from the sounds on the other end that he had just got in the door. He was wandering around his flat, probably getting ready for bed whilst we talked.

'How are you doing?' I asked

'A lot better than you, I hear.'

Ouch. He could tease me because we both knew he cared.

'It's late, what do you want?'

'I want to know about drugs.'

He chuckled, 'Are you sure you've dialled the right number, Joe?'

'Starz. I want to know who the supplier is.'

'You're the second person tonight to ask me that.'

'Who was the first?'

'Pistol Penny.'

'Pistol Penny?' I sat up straight.

I had heard all about her. A Detective Sergeant in South London. According to the news she was part of a long-running task force working to take down a group of top-level drug dealers known as "the Brixton six". They all controlled different territories but worked in collaboration to try and minimise interference from the police and maximise profits. It was every police officer's nightmare, that drug dealers might actually get intelligent.

One day, they were attempting to run surveillance

on an unprecedented meeting of all six. Gunshots were heard, people scattered, and the small unit of officers were all heading in different directions. The Met had not released the exact details of what had happened, but what was known to journalists was that DS Penny Price had taken it on herself to enter the building during this chaos. Then more gunshots were heard.

When armed officers arrived they found DS Price alive, and the Brixton six dead. Hence the nickname, Pistol Penny. She had been cleared of any wrongdoing, but what really happened inside that building was something only she knew.

'She took down the Brixton six,' Andy explained.

'I know who she is, why did she get hold of you?'

'She's our newest DCI.'

It took a moment for the penny to drop. *Shit*.

'What did you tell her?'

'What do you mean, what did I tell her?'

Once a week, Andy's dad, a truly lovely man, comes and sits with him whilst they talk things over. This evening, during one of these sessions, sitting alone in the dark of the basement, well past leaving time, sharing a drink and stories, they heard an announcing cough from behind them.

'DS Watson?'

Andy turned around in mild surprise, 'Yes? What

can I do for you?'

'Erm… I was looking for the Organised Crime Database?'

'That's me.'

The woman visitor raised her eyebrows and stayed standing to attention.

'You're DCI Price.' He smiled, as he always does, 'I remember seeing your photo on the news.'

'If one more person congratulates me—' she started.

'I don't think that's appropriate,' he interrupted.

'Thank you.'

'It's a shame that had to end the way it did.'

'Yes,' she said genuinely, 'It is.'

Andy has a huge, warm smile, and I'm sure he would have deployed it at this moment. 'You need help with something?'

She stood back to attention. 'I was hoping you could brief me.'

'Sure thing, take a seat.'

'I'm ok,' normally she would have ended it there, but apparently his smile earnt him some courtesy, 'Thank you.'

'Whatever's comfortable.' He gestured to his dad, 'This is Harry, by the way.'

Harry, ever the gentleman, stood up to shake her hand.

'Lovely to meet you.'

When stood up, he has a bit of belly, but only because he loves his food and his wine a bit too much. I'd like to get that old and that happy one day. If I end up like Harry I'll know I've made the right decisions in life.

'Yes, you too,' she replied, 'Are you... sorry, I don't know who you are.'

'He's just my dad, it's alright.'

'Your dad?'

'Yeah, he comes down each week and I just run things by him.'

'I see, old hand, are you, Harry?'

'Christ no, he's a jeweller.'

'Down the Lanes,' added Harry, breaking out his warm smile too. He must be where Andy gets it from.

Price couldn't help being won over by their relaxed charm. Apparently she even smiled a bit herself.

'Come on, sit down,' Andy insisted.

With a sigh, and a reluctant smile, she took a seat next to him. He poured a glass of Cointreau and offered it to her.

'I'm carefully ignoring the fact that you're drinking.'

'I clocked off hours ago.'

'Seems everyone did,' she retorted.

He poured the drink into Harry's glass and addressed the issue at hand.

'What is it you want to know?'

What she wanted to know was everything about

starz.

'Starz,' he sighed.

He had given the speech a few times now, which made it easy for him to tell me exactly what he told her.

'It's unbelievable, you change the chemical makeup of a drug and you've got a completely different drug: not covered by current legislation. The formula is similar to amphetamines, so the best guess is it's supposed to be a cheap ADHD drug. Outside of current patents. But instead it's popular with clubbers.'

'That's it?' Price butt in, 'A party drug?'

'The trouble is that if you change the makeup of a drug it most often does something completely different,' he explained. 'In one-out-of-a-hundred cases, if you take more than two, and especially if you're taking some brands of birth control, it leads to internal haemorrhaging. Not pretty. Twenty-three deaths in just the last few months. That constitutes a killing spree. The biggest serial killer the city has ever seen. But instead they call it misadventure. A killer pill. But the people who sell them to teenagers are the real killers.'

Price sat and chewed this over.

He continued, 'One of the first cases was a young girl Joe Grabarz was hired to find. He found her alright.'

'How much did he charge for that pleasure?'

Andy assured me that he gave her a disapproving

look. 'Legal highs are a bitch.'

'Are you sure you want to say that out loud?'

'To you? To dad? I think I'll risk it. In sensible countries they blanket ban any psychoactive substances and make exceptions for alcohol and nicotine. Either that or they legalise everything and then you can regulate the market. Here we just ban specific chemical formulas, meaning that we're always chasing to catch up.'

'You make it sound worse than it is.'

'For a few months, or even years, depending on the size of the problem or how slowly the Home Office works, a new drug is legal, and can even be sold on the high street. In Brighton it's usually Kemptown or North Laine. Legislation hasn't caught up with starz yet. If it becomes a national problem then the government will start to deal with it, but at the moment it's just a Brighton problem, which means *we* have to deal with it.'

She didn't say what she thought about it, she just studied him. Who knows what she thought.

'Don't get me wrong,' he added, 'I'll defend the law however stupid it is, we're the police, that's what we do.' They should put that on the badge, I thought.

'I would drink to that,' she finally responded.

The next question on both of our lips was who had the supply. Who was the bastard behind it all? 'The answer is the same for any drug,' Andy answered,

'Robert Coward. He's a bad bastard, make no mistake. He's more murders to his name than even the pills.'

'Then why haven't you put him away?' she asked.

'Because I can't prove it.'

'Why not?'

'I haven't got any bodies. This poor bastard on the beach is the first one. One shot, so good luck with it.'

'Tell me about him.'

'Dad can probably tell you more than I can.'

'Started as a barrow boy,' Harry spoke for the first time in a while.

'Selling fruit and veg,' Andy explained.

'Not just. If you dug under the runner beans or lifted up the marrows you'd find all sorts. And if you weren't in when they came knocking you'd find half your stuff missing.' He finished and took a sip of Cointreau.

'Keep going,' Price said.

I got the story separately from Harry later on, and below is how he told it to me.

'Bobby is, from the way people talk about him, a real bastard. Pardon my French. A ruthless, old-fashioned gangster. But in all my life I've never crossed paths with gangsters, thankfully. I knew him long before all that. But even then he was an evil sod.

'Now, people usually exaggerate when they use the

word evil. But I mean cold, calculated, pure evil.

'During the war my dad had a greengrocers in Kemptown. When I wasn't in the shop we were all out in the street. Children in them days could run around wherever they wanted. We must have been ten or twelve or thereabouts. It was a strange time. All the young men were slowly disappearing. The older boys at school. Older brothers. The streets were far more empty than they are today. Some people still made deliveries with horse and cart.

'We had a good bunch of friends. We were all the sons of the shop owners. The butcher's son, the baker's son. But not the son of the candlestick maker!'

He laughed a throaty laugh that soon became a cough.

'Our favourite place was down under the arches by the seafront,' he continued. 'During the war they stopped running the Volks Railway partly because some legislation put all public transport into city ownership, which took it out of the original owner's hands, and partly because they were fortifying the beaches in case the Germans crossed the channel. That meant the carriages had to be stored away, and they were stored away under the arches. The Volk's carriages are smaller than a normal carriage as I'm sure you know. But in our games that made us grown-up size. We would be cowboys like in *The Great Train Robbery*, or Buster Keaton in *The General*, always climbing on the roof, almost falling off whilst the train careered out of control across some perilously high bridge over a huge canyon. It was a giant playground where we could spend entire days in our own fantasies.

'My dad was happy to keep me there. He was busy trying to shelter me from the news. The slow realisation that some people were never coming home. He lost a brother. I know now, but I have no memory of ever being told.

'I do have one strong memory that still sticks with me. Our shop was right near the entrance to the tunnels that run all under Kemptown. I mean, they're cellars really, but loads of them connect. I probably remember them bigger than they were. Opposite us was Finlater's the wine merchants, corner of Upper Rock Gardens and St. James Street. It was a lot of people's designated entrance when the bombers came over toward London. You had to have a designated entrance so that you were counted in correctly. We knew we had an hour, maybe an hour and half, before the spitfires and hurricanes would rout them from the London skies and they would head back, dropping anything they had left on us.

'It had hit all the parents pretty hard when those children died in the Odeon bombing, but us children would just run through the tunnels raising hell until we got tired. Some nights the all clear wouldn't sound for hours and we young ones would sleep on the few bunks that were around. I remember one night, pretending to be asleep, watching my father's face as he listened for the low hum of approaching aircraft. With me asleep he didn't have to pretend that everything was alright. I've never forgotten his face like that. I never got to see it again as he died before I got the chance to really know him as an adult.'

At this point Harry took a sip of some very specific Bordeaux he was having. He didn't speak for a few moments.

I steered him back on track: 'Robert Coward?'

He continued, 'One day, when we headed down to the arches we found some other boys playing on the carriages. The oldest of them, a boy my age, was called Bobby. We were happy to share, but Bobby's idea of fun wasn't fun for us. Once too many of us had got hurt, someone suggested that we should play for the rights to the carriages and everyone agreed.

'I had with me my dad's bat and ball, so we decided on a game of cricket. There was five or six of us on each side so it took a while to play. Especially during those summers, when an hour was a day, and a day was a year. A crowd of other children started to gather and watch from the railings of the seafront above us.'

He leant forward, remembering the excitement of the game like it was the Ashes, 'Batting second, they needed ten to beat us, just down to Bobby and the other biggest boy. Any wicket would win it for us, but we only had ten balls left. I was bowler. I was always bowler. It probably wasn't really the last ball, but that's the way it was always told, and that's the way I remember it now. Bobby was in when I bowled a brilliant leg-spin and caught our makeshift stumps. We had won.'

He finished his glass. I bought him another.

'Now I'm not saying that my dad was a saint. But he ran a mostly honest business. He did have a trick of loading two boxes full of identical tomatoes and labelling one as "special tomatoes". Which were obviously twice the price. Halfway through the day, when the special tomatoes had all but gone, it was my job to refill the box with the rest of the "normal" ones.

'I think it must have been the humiliation of being defeated in front of all those other children. But that week Bobby started selling from his dad's barrow, right outside our shop. He lived in Hanover, but wheeled it all that way, as a child, just for revenge. Whatever my dad was selling, he sold cheaper. With no rent to pay, no overheads, he could keep it up as long as he needed to. He was there every day. School started and he stayed. I was evacuated down to Cornwall. Still he stayed. When I came back my dad was out of business. He had kept that from me too.

'I never saw Bobby again, but I heard plenty through the grapevine. First the black market, then housebreaking, racketeering. And when the drugs trade appeared in proper I wasn't surprised to hear he was the first in Brighton to get involved.

'I was lucky, working at Chrome Productions until my lung collapsed. Then into the Jewellery trade. I'd be happy if Andy would just hurry up and give me some grandchildren to spoil.

'My dad ended up at the coal merchants at the end of Riley Road. He never really recovered. Never got to see us have Andy. He was only fifty-eight when he died.'

I could hear down the phone that Andy was now tucked up in bed. His partner, Darren, was mumbling something. It was time for me to get off the phone but I had to ask one more thing.

'Did you tell her about Max?'

'Your mysterious supervillain? I don't want her to think I believe you.'

He laughed, but it wasn't genuine. There was a pause.

'She asked about you though.'

'What did you tell her?'

'The truth.'

'Which is?'

'You're the best.'

I smiled, 'Goodnight, Andy' and hung up.

He really was the best kind of person. Sometimes I wished I could be like that. But I wasn't made that way.

I pried apart the venetian blinds and looked out into the empty Lanes. It had started raining and a sea-mist was creeping into the corridors, creating impenetrable pitch-black, slicked cobbled death-traps. Shutters covered the emptied jewellers' windows. Storm Joseph was fast approaching. I didn't want to have to go back out there. I could just sleep in my office.

I decided that now was a good time to take stock of what I had, if I really was going to do something about this mess. Rory was obviously pushing starz for Coward's men. Something had happened and they had murdered him. No great mystery there. They tried to disguise his identity. And they would have succeeded if it wasn't for me. Did that mean there was something linking Rory to Coward? Something we were bound to find if we looked hard enough?

Where is it!? That was what the big man had screamed at Thalia. Where was what? The package of starz? It was certainly hidden. But there was nothing unusually valuable in that. Unless Rory had done something particularly stupid. Which was a distinct possibility.

I didn't know. What I did know was that the court summons was sitting on my desk. It needed doing something about. I couldn't help Rory, but I could help myself.

Investigate ABC Construction.

ABC Construction, Rory's building. A strange co-incidence. Maybe that's all it was. I needed more information, a proper brief. I punched my desk in frustration, launched up, and threw the summons in the bin. I wouldn't be needing it.

7

Damn Powerful Women

I TOOK A SWIG of the brandy that I kept in my desk for chilly nights. Then I headed down my stairs, stepping over Lenny, who was already asleep, and stepped outside into the cold. Buffeted by the weather, I made it round the corner to my lock-up, and had to fight against the wind to open the shutter door. But soon I was inside my helmet, a million miles from the cold and the damp, and my Honda was purring between my legs, ready to go to work.

When I had done my due diligence on Todman Concrete I had been told that M. Todman, scion of the company's founder, and now owner of the business, was a member of the Chandler Club. This was a snotty-nosed gentlemen's club in the poshest part of Hove. And I mean gentlemen, women are strictly not allowed.

It was around midnight, but it was still worth a shot. These rich business types often seemed to go entirely without sleep, working twenty-four-seven. The reason was an insatiable drive to make money, they would say. But there's a real reason for it. It's called cocaine.

I zoomed through the town, listening to my Honda roar through the twenty-miles-an-hour zone. Flicking the finger at the council. And soon I was across the border into Hove.

How can I describe Hove? Well, imagine a beautiful woman. Gorgeous. Cultured. Everybody loves her. And she's fun too, a bit too much fun sometimes, if you know what I mean. Well, if you can imagine her, then Hove is her perpetually disapproving younger sister. The sort of woman who when mistaken for her sister, "You're Nancy, aren't you?" would reply, "Deborah, actually." And it's that "actually" that sums up Hove.

There's little history to find in the place either, despite the village dating back into the same recesses of time that Brighthelmstone was founded in. This is because of both the blessing and the curse of being so close to Brighton. At the beginning of the nineteenth century the population was recorded as one-hundred-and-one. One-hundred-and-one people, that's all. More people work in your office. Fifty years later it was over four-thousand. And now one-hundred-and-one people live in each of the three, four, or five story town houses that dot First, Second, Third, and Fourth Avenues, between the shops and restaurants, that is. And the rich people now live on Tongdean Road, which is so suburban it'll hurt your eyes to look at it.

All this is due to Hove's only notable quality being that it is nearby, populating it with a strange mix of those who can't afford to live in Brighton, next to those who can afford not to live in Brighton. I don't understand that either, but go to Hove and you'll realise it's true. And let's not forget that, thanks to the railway line, a lot of these were Londoners buying second homes. A crime that continues to this day.

So, history be damned, the old "manor house", such that it was, was demolished, and now a block of flats sits where it was. The whole town became a regency extension, a west wing of Brighton, bodged-up over a few decades.

These days the marriage is official, it's Brighton & Hove. But in my heart, in everyone's hearts, it's still Brighton *and* Hove. The houses and the squares I was bombing past looked lovely, no doubt, but they were built just as stables to keep rich people in. And now they're stables for rich people to keep poor people in.

All that said, and despite all my cynicism, I'd still trade everything I have for one day in regency Brighton. Even regency Hove. Hell, even regency Shoreham.

I headed along Church Road until it becomes New Church Road, where Hove slowly transitions into its quieter fringes. Five minutes later, I was parked up in the shadow of the imposing stone building. It almost looked as if it was carved out of a single piece of heavy granite, protruding up from the very bowels of the earth. This was of course an illusion, everything is chalk down here, so some ancient civilisation must have erected it at some point. Heaven knows what the building was originally, although knowing how old the club was, it could easily have been built for it.

To the public the outside bore no sign to inform you of what was inside. That was the way they wanted it, of course. If you didn't know it was there then you had no business finding out.

There was absolutely no one on the pavement now, the wind was getting too strong, and if people had hatches to batten down, they were doing it. But I was working, lucky me.

I have never felt scruffier than when I walked inside those doors. The way the guy on the reception desk's eyes bulged when he saw me I might have been a marauding crackhead about to chow-down on his limbs. He was wearing a tuxedo with tails for Christ's sake, and he just worked here.

He had a head that fondly remembered wisps of grey hair, in fact he was grey all over, he could have been manning the desk since the club was founded.

Without lunch breaks, from the look of him. At the top of his thin frame was an enormous flat nose, which gave him an unfair advantage when looking down it at people like me. Coupled with an almost imperceptibly long face, he looked like a knackered old horse that had been kicked every day of its life.

When his surprisingly active blue eyes fixed firmly on me, without blinking, I lied, and told him that I was invited. He looked as though he sincerely doubted that fact. But after I said it again, louder this time, he scurried off to find the Concrete Prince. Either that or he was using it as a pretence to get help. He could be phoning the police right now.

I used the time to take a look at the lobby. It was at least two stories high, with marble columns. Coats of arms and ancient looking lances and pikes decked the walls. There was plush, blood-red carpet covering the far half, leading into the club, and a brass borderline separating it from the bare stone floor I was standing on. This threshold was not to be crossed by the likes of me. This place was a traditional, historic, cigar-smoking, button-back leather institution for elitism, misogyny, and conservative values. Even the smell of the place was thick with privilege.

The man reappeared more swiftly than I thought he would, and braver than I expected.

'Who did you say invited you?' he commanded me to answer.

Not again. 'Mr Todman!' I pretty much shouted.

'There's no Mr Todman, sir.'

Was this guy an idiot? 'Todman Concrete.'

'I see.'

He frowned at my clothes and gave me a look that suggested he knew something I didn't, like I was a child with chocolate on my face pretending I hadn't eaten any cake.

'I will tell *Miss* Todman that you are here.' He dropped that bomb and marched off.

Miss Todman? But the Chandler Club was men-only, I was sure of it. Did they allow female guests? Maybe. But I was told Todman was a member.

A couple more minutes later, the man reappeared and I was led not over the threshold, but to a side room. The sign above it said "Non-members". At the Chandler Club there are no guests, no visitors, just non-members. He left me alone and I sank into a heavy brown leather chair. The room appeared to be built entirely of dark wood, as though we were inside a hollowed out walnut tree. They had clearly made the decision that all the furniture and furnishings could range anywhere between black and brown, but nowhere outside that short spectrum. One entire wall was covered in bookshelves, packed with those military textbooks, encyclopedias, and editions of Hansard that look nice but that no one ever actually wants to read. There appeared to be a small, fold out bar hidden in the middle of them. I felt like helping myself, not because I particularly wanted a drink, but because they wouldn't want me to. But the thought struck me that whoever this Concrete Countess was, she was suing me. I should probably do at least the minimum possible to get on her good side.

Opposite my chair was an empty partner. Clearly this room was for sitting down with non-members, getting them pliant, and then telling them to leave quietly.

You had to stare at something for a few moments before your eyes could really see it. The dulcet light came from an array of lamps and wall fittings, every one behind a shade so that each seemed to throw the dim glow of a single candle in different directions, giving the room the soft, seductive quality of a love nest. Or maybe that was just my imagination.

Eventually the door opened, being held by the horse-faced man. I heard that sexy clacking of heels, god I love that sound, and my unremarkable eyes, which have never asked for much, experienced the best image they have ever been treated to. Appearing through the half-light, first a pair of oil-black heels, painfully high, then legs that looked like they would reach above my head.

In strutted a siren, a beautiful older woman. I say older, she must have been about fifty, so well within my range, if you know what I mean. She was stunning, filling out an elegant black dress that didn't reveal anything, but suggested everything. Too much everything.

She floated down into the other chair, she was even classier than the surroundings, and without deigning to introduce herself, smile, or even make eye contact, addressed me.

'Would you like a drink?'

Her voice was like pouring honey down my throat. And there was an accent there, something enchantingly subtle that I couldn't place.

'A Negroni,' I said to the man. It was clear that my answer was to be made to the staff, not her.

He nodded, and turned his head towards her, ready for her order.

'A brandy Old Fashioned with brown sugar,' she said, and he seemed to glide backwards out of the room.

A brandy Old Fashioned with brown sugar? That sounded nice. I would have to try one of them sometime.

Silence returned to the room. I studied the woman opposite. I felt like I had been given a private showing of a Botticelli. Except Botticelli painted blondes. He didn't know what he was missing. She had olive-coloured skin. Long, straight, oil-black hair. And full, round, blood-red lips.

We were alone. Me and this woman. I wanted to

take a bite out of her, she looked delicious. I guess she could afford to.

'This is cosy,' I said to break the silence.

'They won't let you in the club dressed like that.'

I smirked, but she didn't return it. She still wasn't looking at me, clearly I wasn't interesting enough for her.

'I thought this place was men only.'

'It is,' was all she offered in the way of an explanation.

Finally, she looked at me, and I wished she hadn't. She had enormous, emerald green eyes nestled beneath smoky lids and thick lashes. The effect finished her face off perfectly like a great piece of jewellery. I was going again. Powerful women. Damn powerful women.

'So M. Todman of Todman Concrete is…?

'Monica.'

I nodded to myself, busy recalibrating everything I had expected and planned for this meeting, whilst trying to fight against the haze she was creating.

The man returned with our drinks and delivered them to our side tables without a word. He left again, never turning his back on her. She was business royalty after all.

She took a mouthful. Her glass was dripping with condensation. It wasn't the only one.

'Tell me, Monica, why does someone spend more

money suing someone than they could ever bleed them for?'

'Because a reputation is worth more.'

'Is that right?'

'And…' she gave a little playful smirk, 'to give them a kick up the arse.'

The smirk was like catnip. On top of everything, she was playful. A playful, powerful woman. I needed to hold it together. Another part of my brain was telling me I needed to get laid. I really needed to get laid. Shut up, brain. Not right now. Another time.

'I hired you, Joseph, for your legendary services. But you did a poor job.'

'No one calls me Joseph,' I said calmly.

'No one calls me Monica.'

Could she tell I was attracted to her? Of course she could, I was practically on fire. I took a sip of my drink to try and relax me. It was a good Negroni.

'Another detective once told me, if you don't like the answers you're getting, you're asking the wrong questions. "Investigate ABC Construction" isn't much of a brief.'

She leant forward to give a snappy response, but then leant back again, as though she thought better of it. She tapped her heels on the floor for a few beats, and then took a gulp of her drink. A drop of condensation dripped onto her neck and ran all the way down out of sight. Lucky sod.

I waited for her, taking a sip of my drink to pass the time. Eventually she put the Old Fashioned down and leant forward again, her hands together, ready to talk shop.

'The new flats they're building down in the Marina are the biggest development in the city for decades. ABC is building the first phase in what will be eight-hundred units. They came to us for the concrete contract. You can't imagine what that is worth. Then, a few months ago, suddenly ABC makes a big show of ripping up all our work and bringing in French contractors. French concrete.' She said that last part like it was the worst insult possible.

I knew all this already. 'I told you what they told me: they just weren't happy with your work. They needed a higher grade mix.'

'So they say,' she retorted.

'So they say, what more do you want?'

'I want you to do some detecting!' Her playfulness had gone now. She was every inch the ruthless businessperson I had heard about. 'I started in this business when I was fourteen, Mr Grabarz, mixing the concrete with my father. Back when my father *was* the business. I know concrete. We don't meet the requirements, we exceed them.'

I shrugged, not knowing what she wanted. 'So they're idiots.'

'Idiots who have severely damaged my reputation.'

'So sue them, you're good at it.'

'To sue I need evidence.'

Finally, I understood my purpose in this whole scheme. She wanted to prove that they had ripped up their work for a different reason, because that turned their statement about the quality of their concrete into slander. She could sue them for that. And once she had sued them for that, then she could sue them for loss of revenues, or something else like that. I was sure she would try. *If* they had a different reason, that was.

'What if there's nothing to find?'

'We delivered that order of concrete in sixteen trucks, they delivered theirs in twenty-two. Please explain that.'

I thought about it. Wanting, of course, to eliminate the obvious.

'Smaller trucks?'

'Very slightly smaller capacity. Accounts for one truck. Still leaves five extra.'

'And in your personal opinion, as someone who knows concrete, there's no reason for that.'

'Nothing legitimate. And I mean that exactly how it sounds. They've been getting these deliveries every couple of weeks since.'

'Are they over by the same amount?'

'I wouldn't know, we were never contracted for those orders. I can only tell you about the first one. I've no reason to think that they are, and no reason to think that they aren't.'

I sat back for a moment, sipping my drink and having a good old think. Was there something else inside those trucks? Something smuggled in. Something illegal. It seemed the obvious reason, and I'm sure she thought that too. But she couldn't break windows or break heads. Private Detectives are only hired for three reasons: either the police are not interested, or there's no crime involved, or it requires committing a crime. Did I really want to expose myself to that kind of risk, with the police on my back already, just for five measly grand? If I was smarter I'd know I was doing it for those legs. Plus everything else on top.

'Did ABC pay you?'

'This isn't about money,' she said quickly.

'Listen, Monica, my job is made a lot easier when people just answer my questions. That goes double for clients.'

She chewed her tongue. She might not like me telling her what to do, but she knew it was in her best interests. Which is why I knew I could get away with it. Which is why I did it. Because, let's face it, I enjoyed doing it.

'Yes,' was the little she wanted to give me.

'In full?'

'Yes.'

'After the job was finished?'

'The last of it, yes. So what? If you're worried about

my legal position—'

'I'm really not worried about that,' I interrupted. 'I was just wondering why they would pay you if they were unhappy,' I continued, 'unless they suddenly needed to be unhappy.'

She leant back in her chair, not entirely understanding what I meant. Maybe I didn't either.

Then she said, 'I intend to destroy this coward.' She meant it too.

'It's not *the* most cowardly thing I've heard,' I added, not really meaning anything, but she looked at me as though I was stupid.

'That's his name,' she explained, 'Robert Coward.'

I sat up straight.

'The C in ABC,' she added.

Well, this changed things. Dramatically. I took it completely seriously now.

'Some extra trucks isn't much to go on.'

She sighed, 'I went to you because I couldn't go to the police. And when the police can't go to the police they go to you. What is it they see in you?'

It was my turn to smirk. 'Dirty hands.'

8

Concrete Evidence

I FINISHED MY NEGRONI, and bid the alluring Miss Todman a good night. In the lobby I almost made the man's eyes pop out of his head by placing one foot over the brass threshold. I couldn't resist.

'I had something on my shoe.'

Frowning, he said 'I hope you had an enjoyable evening, Mr Grabarz.' He just wanted me to know he had my name.

'Thanks for the warm welcome,' I sarcastically threw back at him.

He seemed to sincerely not care, and went back to whatever it was he did when there was no one around. I headed out into the cold.

It was getting chilly again now, like being trapped in a freezer. The sky was a grey curtain pulled over the city, and the wind was spiking erratically, harbingering the storm that I could see approaching from the horizon, over the sea. From France. There seemed to be no better time to "investigate ABC Construction" than right now.

I jumped on my bike and roared back along New Church Road, then Church Road, then across the border back into Brighton, through the town centre, and out the other side. I was buffeted by the wind as I emerged up onto the coast road heading east toward the marina. Everything below cliff height was now shrouded in a sea mist that was settling over the strange ghost town that is the marina at night. I zipped the wrong way down the Marina Way off ramp and circled down the long flyover into the fog.

The marina has restaurants, cafés, pubs, a cinema, a bowling alley, some flats, and a Chinese restaurant on a boat. But no clubs. The only thing open that late is the casino. And it's not a big one.

My Honda gently hummed through the thick fog, just in case there was a gambling patron lurking somewhere around, but I parked up without seeing a soul. In this mist I was only going to see someone if they were within ten feet of me, and given that everything else was shut the odds seemed very unlikely. Maybe Miss Todman had arranged this weather especially for my illicit activities, it seemed within her power.

I marched toward the construction site feeling unnervingly blind. My footsteps made no noise audible above the squall, which was good for stealth, but also meant that there could be an army of zombies just eleven feet away and I would never hear them coming.

The site was appearing gradually out of the grey haze. Waves were breaking over the marina wall and lashing what was only the shell of a building. A four-storey concrete shell with long metal fronds extending upwards toward where the rest of the building would be. It was imposing nonetheless, a concrete cliff face above a sea of smoke, and surrounded by a sturdy metal fence a couple of metres high. I say sturdy, but the wind could have ripped it down if it tried.

Brighton marina is apparently the largest marina complex in Europe, whatever that means, but it's set to get even larger. This shell I was approaching was the first of what will be eight or so buildings, one of which will be a forty-storey skyscraper. Cover any old parts on the artist's impression of the finished project and you could be mistaken for thinking it was Dubai or Shanghai. Not little old Brighton.

The increase in population to the marina from eight-hundred new flats was going to be incredible. There was no way of knowing what effect it would have. But then again, what was there to lose here any-way?

I stared through the tall metal fence. There was a single dark opening, which I assumed would one day be a posh glass double door into a lobby. Right now it looked more like the mouth of a cave. My primal instincts were echoing at the back of my skull, *do not go in*.

Outside the entrance, I could see an abandoned cement mixer. A Portakabin site office, lights off. Various tools strewn around. Coupled with the eerie fog, the general impression was that some panic or disaster had happened, everything had been dropped where it was, and the place had been abandoned in a hurry. Maybe it was those zombies.

That was just the cold down my spine talking. Really, the workmen were just lazy, I told myself. I wondered if there was a guard. The Portakabin lights were definitely off. Still, he could be walking around. I could handle a guard, you can always buy them. But cameras? I hoped not. If her hunch was right then this place was being used for some shady stuff, and I was pretty sure they wouldn't want cameras in that case. But they *would* want a guard. Can you always buy a guard if he's working for a ruthless bastard criminal? Also, I didn't have any money. *I want to go home*, I thought. Anywhere warm would do. So, I'd better do this quickly.

I hauled myself over the fence, and sloshed through dirty puddles. The Portakabin was locked. I had taken a hefty torch from one of my saddlebags but I didn't want to attract attention out here. I knelt down to pick the lock in the dark. It didn't take long.

Although it had looked sturdy on the outside, inside I could hear every wall and panel rattling. I wouldn't want to be in here when Storm Joseph hit. I flicked on the torch, but with my own special invention on the end: a piece of white cloth attached with a rubber band. A diffuser of sorts that gave me a two-foot bubble of smooth light, rather than a narrow, mile-long beam that would show in the fog like a laser through smoke, and probably land small aircraft in the process.

Despite my intelligence, there was nothing in the cabin to find. Just hard hats, high-vis jackets, and a shitload of mud. I guess they weren't quite lazy enough to leave important stuff lying around. I clicked off the torch. The cabin rattled again. Smatterings of rain lashed the tiny windows. The wind was making it through the gaps around the frame, playing that harmonica-of-the-damned sound that it does through your letterbox at night. Like blowing across the mouth of a bottle. It could be the call of some ghost ship out in the storm. Calling me out there to Davy Jones' locker. I wasn't swimming to France in this weather. And there was nothing here. That only left me one option: the mouth of the cave and the darkness within.

Once inside the shell, and despite all my primal instincts, I was still surprised just how dark it was. I needed the full beam in here. It was darker than outside and even noisier. The outside walls were wrapped in plastic sheeting, which was valiantly fighting to keep out the storm. As it slapped and whipped against the scaffolding I felt like I was inside a giant Christmas present desperately being torn at by an excited child. But the plastic was winning, despite the occasional rip it was still protecting me.

What it couldn't keep out was the mist. It was as thick inside the corridors as it had been outside, rendering the torch and all its beam practically useless. The only purpose it served was to warn me of the random, and very dangerous, drops in the floor that were waiting to be filled by lift shafts. I narrowly missed one and caught the reflection from my torch of still-wet concrete. Rain was leaking in through the temporary roof cover four storeys above and dripping in a long shower down the shaft and into the basement. Was it only the surface of the concrete that was wet?

I stepped around the shaft and kept moving deeper into the building. Into its dark heart. There was a room at the end of this corridor, I could just about make out.

Metre by metre I approached, but my torchlight never revealed anything. It was a black hole, light could not escape it. Then it became more like a black haze, the sheen of the air moisture repelling a slight glow.

At last, I stepped inside. It was much quieter in here. The storm was just a memory, something that can't touch you when surrounded by concrete on all six sides. It felt like an empty bank vault. A safe deposit box. Maybe it was.

Across the floor of the room were wooden pallets. Most of them were broken, a few were still intact. Only one of them was loaded. I could feel my heartbeat increasing. If there was something to find, this was it.

I pulled out my penknife, which *is* a tool apparently, and cut through the tarp that was lashed over it. Small boxes toppled out. Small prescription pill boxes. I picked one up, ripped the foil covered plastic tray out, and popped a pill into my hand. Blue. Round. With a star debossed in the centre. I looked at the packet. I couldn't read it. Not just because it was dark and it was mostly chemistry. But because it was in French.

I pocketed it and marched back down the corridor. I had to do something about this. But what could that be? At the very least, getting the police involved would give Monica Todman her case for suing ABC and get her off my back. The police would set up surveillance and start adding faces to the names on Andy's wall. Beyond that I could be pretty sure nothing would touch Robert Coward. He wouldn't know anything about it. People like him are always just out of reach.

I started to jog through the puddles and round the lift shafts. But what was there to charge them with anyway? All we could prove was that their premises were used to store some drugs that aren't illegal anyway. Damn legal highs. Fuck 'em.

A harsh metal clang!

I froze. Adrenaline was remorselessly injected into my bloodstream. I turned off the torch. All I could hear was the storm tearing at the plastic. Rainwater dripping through the layers of the building. I had been too busy thinking to pay attention. What had it sounded like? Metal, definitely. Metal on metal? Perhaps something had blown over. Either way, every nerve in my body was telling me to run down the corridor, vault the fence in one leap, and ride my bike as fast as I could.

I overrode them. Steadily moving one foot in front of the other. Back down the corridor, keeping the torch off this time.

It all happened in a second. I heard a scrabbling sound, like claws on a wood floor, then felt a blinding pain in the side of my head. I was falling. Everything was red, like my own head was closing up around me. Then it got ten times worse. Things went dark. Thick liquid started pouring into every orifice. Eyes. Ears. Mouth. I was drowning. Drowning in something thick, viscous, that I could barely kick against. With a dawning terror I realised what had happened. Someone had struck me with something, sent me plummeting down a lift shaft into what was definitely still-wet concrete.

I surfaced. Gasping for air, but not getting any. Struggling to stay up. I went under again. Up again. I couldn't see, my face was plastered shut with the stuff. I dragged myself in any direction. Slapping, smacking at the stuff, trying to get traction. My energy was already giving out. I didn't have anything left. My heart, arms, and legs felt like they were on fire. If I gave up I was going under again and I wouldn't make it back up this time.

Finally, I hit something solid. Pulled myself out with the very last of my strength. I lay there, oxygen barely entering my lungs through a mouth and nostrils that were clogged with slowly solidifying building material.

Footsteps. My brain screamed at me that I was not alone. *Get up! Get up!* I ran blindly towards the sound of rain. I felt it on my skin a few seconds before I ran straight into the fence. I fumbled for it, managed to wrench myself over it.

What happens to concrete if you swallow it? If it gets in your ears? Your eyes? Your skin? Was someone going to find me tomorrow, frozen solid like one of those lame human statues? Dead. I needed to get the stuff off me. But how? I could only hear one thing: waves.

I turned in the direction where I thought the moorings were and jumped. I fell again. For what seemed like a terrifyingly long time. Then I hit the water. It felt as solid as concrete when I broke through it. But it was unmistakably, undeniably, painfully cold. I thrashed and thrashed, eyes open, I had to clean even my eyeballs, and when I could thrash no more I surfaced. I could see. I was only five metres from a jetty.

When I pulled myself out I collapsed onto the floor in the foetal position. Shivering. To add insult to injury the wind was making it through every gap in my clothes. Round my neck. Down my back. Up my back. I would be a frozen ice-sculpture instead. It was this wind that got me back up again. Running, desperate, for my bike.

You may think that a situation like this was no time for pride, but there was just no way that I could let Thalia see me like that. Especially after being so selfish toward her. It would just be too humiliating. I needed somewhere warm. Somewhere to shower. Some clean clothes. The answer was obvious: Rory's.

I fumbled the key into the lock and pushed. The door had definitely got heavier since I was last here. I flicked on the torch, the white beam adding to the sterile atmosphere.

As I went about closing every curtain and pulling down every blind I surveyed the carnage left by the CSI team. The sofa was stripped down to its frame. The covers missing. And the cushions bagged up in the corner. All the floorboards leading from the sofa to the door were missing. They were thorough, I'd give them that.

It looked as though a few items had been removed. But then again, it looked that way last time. It was just so sparse, I couldn't remember if they had been there in the first place. There was plastic sheeting covering everything that was left. It looked as though Rory had gone away for ten years and the place was being preserved. But he wasn't coming back, and all this stuff would be landfill soon enough.

In the bathroom I got the shower running and it started to fill the room with a lovely hot steam as I peeled off my clothes. They were stiff and made an uncomfortable cracking noise from the already dry concrete residue. They were ruined. No argument there.

In the mirror I rooted around in my hair, pulling out tiny grey lumps with hairs attached. I could see a large bruise forming across the side of my face. I didn't know what I had been hit with. Or by whom. But they had done some damage. I've never been handsome, but until then I had never been ugly either. I got by with a chin you could set your watch to and a smile you could punch.

The steam was getting too nice now, soothing my muscles and making me sleepy. I could feel myself being pulled down towards the plush bath mat that was poking through my toes. It was only a bath mat, but my god, in this situation it felt like a king size mattress with duck down pillows.

I leant on the sink. My legs were giving way. I needed to sit down. I *needed* to sit down. Looking around there was nowhere in the bathroom, not even a cabinet of any sort. *The toilet in the other room.* I almost ran. As I collapsed down on the closed plastic lid I heard it crack.

I was so tired. I hadn't slept since George's stupid text. That was probably only twenty-one hours ago, but it felt much longer. It felt like I had been awake for a week.

I was so desperate for it that it filled me with dread to imagine the police were watching the place, and that they would see the lights on. Or otherwise the people in the flat below would call them thinking I had broken in. Either way, people would come breaking down the door just to stop me sleeping. It distressed me so much that I pushed the toilet door shut. Darkness. Sweet, wonderful darkness. There was a lock. At the very least that way it would take them time to get in.

I think I got a couple of hours. Whatever it was it wasn't enough. When I woke it was just starting to get light. I could hear a shower running. Shit. I had left that on. Oh well, who cares. What were they going to do? I doubted Rory would be paying his water bill any more.

With the morning light beginning to fill the tiny

cubicle I could see the inside of the door for the first time.

I felt like I had been punched in the stomach. On it was a collage of photos. Of me. Some of them were photos of me and Rory when we were young. I recognised a couple from birthday parties. One of us in a classroom. The one a photographer had done from the end of secondary school.

But a few of them were recent. Clearly taken with a long lens. Without my knowledge. Without my consent. What the fuck was Rory doing spying on me!?

I was awake now.

9

It Was Real to Us

I RIPPED DOWN the most recent-looking photo, which was me looking unhappy stepping out of an office building off North Road, near-ish the station. Some blustering macho recruitment manager had hired me to find out if his wife was having an affair. She was. With another woman. And I got some pretty good photos of it. When I showed him he tried to punch me. Accused me of spying on his wife. What the hell did he think he was paying me for? Then he accused me of faking the pictures. As if I would know how, I don't even own a computer. He refused to pay, so I held him down and took the money from his wallet. Desperate times and all.

The photo was me coming out of his office. To think that Rory watched it all happen and even took photos, really pissed me off.

I rooted through his wardrobe, threw on some of his clothes, not having any choice, and stormed out of the flat. His neighbours didn't seem to be awake yet. No one had seen me arrive, no one saw me leave.

Outside, the streets were full of rubbish, strewn with wheelie bins and recycling boxes thanks to Storm Joseph. There were some branches in the road too. I couldn't see any trees so god knows how far they had travelled.

Still fuming, I jumped on my bike, rode hard, and practically kicked down my own door.

'Thalia!?' I bellowed.

She came out of the bedroom, not wearing much. It was still early and she was just getting up.

'Where have you been?' She was concerned rather than angry, 'What happened to your face!?'

I brandished the photo, 'You had better be able to explain this?'

She took it from me. 'This looks recent,' was all she said. She was too busy looking at me instead, 'Have you changed your clothes?'

'Don't change the subject.'

'Aren't those Rory's?'

'What the hell was your brother doing taking photos of me!?'

She looked, I suppose genuinely, incredulous, 'Why would I know?'

'You saw him regularly enough.'

'I don't know, Joe. Ok?'

'How can I believe you?'

She didn't like that. Not at all. She was insulted by it. I saw her cool and put on that air of superiority that women do so well.

'Do yourself a favour and shut up before I decide not to tell you something.'

I simmered down.

She told me that her mum had called less than ten minutes ago. I knew her mobile was out of battery, and there was no way my old charger would fit her modern phone, so Thalia must have given her the landline number, I certainly hadn't.

Apparently DCI Price had banged on Elaine's door at seven in the morning looking for information. Information about me of all people. I could see what she was thinking: I knew the victim, I went to the crime scene, I found the drugs. Maybe she thought I was far too involved, that I must be tangled up in it somehow. I felt tangled up, just retroactively. Either that or she was still trying to figure out how I recognised him three-days-bloated and without a face. I was assured that Elaine had told her nothing. I tried to believe that.

The next thing she had pressed her for though was far more interesting. Was there anywhere special to Rory? Interesting question. But Price had gone on to make a big mistake. Either Elaine had given her too many options, or she gave her nothing at all, so Price had gotten more specific. Somewhere you could hide something, she had asked. A good detective never asks you the question they want answered, they ask the other question, they ask you something you don't want to answer and you just tell them what they want to know instead. You think you're being clever.

Where is it!? That's what they wanted from Thalia. And now Price wanted the same thing from Elaine. I didn't even know what they were looking for. But I had the home advantage. I only knew one place that was special to Rory. Special to both of us. Probably best to start there.

Just inside the gates, standing on the knee-cutting tarmac playground, on the outside, that particular shade of red brick was still the same. There are no other bricks quite that colour. The stone steps worn down in the same places. The same railings still broken. It was stuck in time, unable to change. It had been like that for generations before me, and would be the same for generations to come. The same pressure, the same misery, the same desperate attempts to escape.

Never let it be exaggerated, the unusual sensation of walking into your old school. Your brain will tell you that the place has shrunk. You cannot help feeling inferior. It was here that you were chastised, bullied, never respected. Maybe it doesn't feel that way if you were one of the spineless sociopaths who were popular at school, but I wouldn't know.

I shuffled in the entrance and up to the reception desk, feeling everything above, but hiding it well. The receptionist, an ugly old woman who was carrying a lot of weight in what seemed to be the most inconvenient places, probably hired for her inherent ability to terrify children, looked at me over her glasses, suspicious before I had even said a word. I was probably giving off the same scent the kids did.

'Hi there,' I spoke quickly, 'I'm with the council water department. A few of the homeowners whose properties back onto the field have been complaining about flooding because of the high ground water, I'm just going to check out your side.' I dropped onto the desk a business card that read "Steven Burke, Brighton & Hove City Council".

And with that, I was off. As I moved down the corridor I could hear her calling, 'Sir? Sir!? You have to sign in!' but I was already too far away for her to catch me.

The first classroom I passed was the first I had ever been in. Reception. Four-years-old. It was where I met Rory. I had already started and not made any friends. But then some time into the year, it was probably only a couple of weeks but I couldn't remember exactly, six or so students were added to our class. I don't remember if they were new to the school, or just the class, but they were lined up at the front and introduced.

As they went down the line our eyes met. I know that sounds like love at first sight. In a way it was, but it was a love of mischief at first sight. You can tell a naughty kid just by looking at them. Their eyes are always scanning. Looking for an opportunity. Rory was scanning the room for a potential accomplice, and I met the requirements.

Naughty kids are often class clowns, often bullies. We were neither. In fact we were the ones laughed at, the ones bullied. Bullied for being weird, for not liking the same things as everyone else. For not being able to afford the same things as everyone else. I lived off charity and Rory's parents didn't earn much. We were both in permanently dirty clothes. Faded, ripped, hand-me-downs. With holes you could poke your fingers through. Holes that the wind and the rain got through. The kids in the current class looked much happier than we had. They were all talking, the nice-looking woman teacher was running through some mnemonic to help them remember something or other. The classroom was a lot more colourful than I remember it being in our day. But maybe that was just my memories. If you can see the past through rose-tinted glasses, I'm sure you can see it through grey-tinted ones too. I went down past the music room, right at the broken fire extinguisher, left at the strange papier-mâché statue. As I passed one wall I noticed behind a Plexiglas screen a picture of some students performing in a school play. One of them was someone I knew, which meant the display hadn't been changed since I was there. That was a bloody long time. The rest of the walls were covered in posters for events that had long finished, and health and safety advice that was probably now out of date. We used to call it "poster blindness". There was so much that you never noticed any of it. If you ever have something that you desperately want to keep secret, print it as a poster and put it on a school wall. No one will ever read it.

I stopped at the "small hall" as we called it. Because it was a hall, and it was smaller than the main hall, obviously. The best two days of my entire school-life had been spent in here. It was junior school, we were sitting in class, as normal, expecting a normal day, when we were told that we were going to the small hall. We assumed it was an assembly, they always seemed to appear out of nowhere.

When we got to the small hall, the headmaster was there. So far, so assembly. Except that all the benches and all the gymnastics equipment, the horse, beanbags, hoops, etc. had been arranged in some unusual, but also symmetrical formation. Was this some new game? Like benchball, or pirates, only far more complicated? No, apparently this was the Santa Maria, and we were the crew of Christopher Columbus, who was the headmaster. Over the next two days we proceeded to load up the ship, and then set sail, looking for the western route to Asia.

Those who seemed to get the most into it were chosen to be officers, and were given the enviable task of supervising the rest of us. Rory did a convincing impression of loading barrels of brandy onto the ship by pretending to craftily tap one and have a swig. This theft, which would earn fifty lashes on any other ship, impressed Columbus so much that he was promoted to First Mate. Thank heavens, otherwise I would have had no one to protect me.

Crewmembers who committed mistakes were given imaginary lashes, the real punishment of which was walking the length of the ship to get the lashes whilst the rest of the crew shouted abuse at them at the top of their lungs. In character, I should say, and encouraged by the head.

On the second day, several months into our voyage, the Captain announced that someone had left the lid off the cured pork, which meant that a large amount of the ship's food supply was ruined. This news was devastating. Would we even have enough food to make land? Would we starve to death?

It was the officers' job to find out who the lax crewmember was, and then punish them. Desperate for some of the attention that Rory was getting, I owned up to the mistake, off-hand, to someone in a small group. The news spread around the ship in seconds.

The rumour was on everybody's lips. Apparently it was Joe.

It was almost the end of the day and thankfully there was no time left to punish me. I've no idea what Rory would have done. The head announced that we had to return to our classrooms now, it was all over, and tomorrow would be just a normal day.

As we trudged back to the classroom, I got some of the dirtiest looks that I have ever been given. Some part of them really believed that I had done it: left the imaginary lid off the imaginary pork, ruining the imaginary food store on the imaginary ship, endangering the imaginary expedition. A crime that the headmaster had made up just to get us even further into it.

But when you're young, fantasies are that potent. You can live in them. We had lived on that ship. It was real to us. Especially during those school days, when an hour was a day, and a day was a year.

You can live in fantasies as an adult, mind, but because they're closer to reality they're harder to spot.

I turned right at the small hall and exited the building by the double doors. Even the field was smaller. When we were young, to be at the other end of it was to be in another country. Miles away from anyone.

It was shared between the primary school and the secondary school, which was next door, so this field had been our playground from five to sixteen. At the end of lunch the caretaker blew a strange bugle/horn type thing, the sound of which carried across the field, across the mountains and rivers of our minds. All the way to the imaginary land we were in. Untouchable. The sound was the only thing that could travel.

Bordering the field was a thicket of trees and bushes. This was where we spent all of our time. Running, climbing, fighting. So many things had happened in here. So many things that I couldn't tell anyone. I remember we kissed once. We just wanted to know what it felt like, people were always doing it in films. Who else could we ask? We didn't have any girl friends, and the only person we trusted that much was each other. I think we even kissed a few times after that, I'm not sure why those ones were. It was kind of nice, sort of soft. I wondered if he remembered that. Then I remembered he was dead. So, no. No he didn't.

I passed a tiny bush, barely as high as my waist. Recognising it, I peered down into it. It seemed hardly bigger than my head inside, but when we had first played in here, it had been our base. Our house. The game we played most often was to go out hunting dinosaurs and come back and cook them. I assume we were cavemen. Not historically accurate, I know. In another fantasy we were ancient warriors, battling against some all-powerful arch-villain who stalked us at every turn. The danger outside the safety of this bush had felt real. It was real to us. Back then it had been big enough to fit us both comfortably inside. It didn't seem to me now that that was possible, but I remembered it that way.

As we had got older and bigger, we had needed a bigger base. This was where I was headed now. I ducked under bushes, stepped over tree stumps, following a well-worn path. Through cobwebs, over anthills. The outside was still intact. A web of threaded branches concealing an inner sanctum. It was our best attempt at building a den. A safe place. Our place.

Misery escaped through fantasy. That had been junior school. But secondary school was something much worse. Forced out of our fantasies most of the time, we were probably still naughty. We hadn't grown out of it. I'm not sure I've grown out of it now.

It's a cliché to suggest that naughty kids are naughty because they're not challenged by what they're learning. Mostly it's not true in my experience, mostly they're just arseholes. Or at least they've been raised by arseholes. I'm not sure what my excuse was. Or is. But Rory *was* genuinely smart. I used to copy his answers. That got me through all of primary school and half of secondary, it was only when we started taking exams, that I couldn't cheat, that I decided school wasn't for me. Without me holding him back he could do really well, he even won the electronics prize that was contested between a few different schools. College was beckoning. University. Maybe a good university. And then a good, cushy job. A wife, kids, death. All done. But he discovered marijuana. And that was that.

I muddied my knees crawling into the den through our designated entrance. More like a cat flap. I was too big now and could hear bits snapping. Once inside I was amazed quite how shit our handiwork was, I remembered it being a lot sturdier than it was. With less holes. I could see everything outside the den, and I was sure anyone could see in. What had been the point of it? Realising that it had survived over fifteen years of rain, storms, and other children, made me feel a bit better.

The place was built around a tree stump that served as our table-come-holy-shrine. The place where we swore our blood oath. We had carved our symbol into it. I scratched away fifteen years of moss and mud. It was still there. You couldn't see it. But you could feel it. The feeling of finding it after all those years, of running my fingers over it again, was almost erotic.

At the base of the stump, where the roots had withered and died, there was a cavity. You couldn't spot it by eye, but there had always been a cavity. When a bully or a teacher wanted something from us. When they would break open our lockers, tip out our bags, even turn us upside down and shake us, this is where we had stashed it.

I reached inside. If anything, this was bigger than I remembered. I still had to feel around to find stuff.

Amongst the bits of dried roots and the flint and the chalk, there was definitely something in there.

Footsteps! Crunching, splashing footsteps announced the presence of heavy-footed intruders. Soon the branches were being ripped from the outside. They had withstood fifteen years, but now they were just kindling.

I sat calmly on the stump, my feet covering the entrance to the cavity. And soon several pairs of burly arms, dark short-haired heads, and one blonde head came into view. She was close behind. She was always very close behind. I'd give her that.

As they ripped down the final barrier between me and them I gave them a quizzical smile, as though I lived in this hovel and really had no idea what they were doing here.

'Everything ok?' I asked.

Price was doubled over, panting. She must have been running.

'Search his pockets,' was all she said.

10

As Slippery as Wet Soap

THEY PULLED EVERYTHING from my pockets. Then they handcuffed me, and bundled me into the back of their panda car. Price was in the other car and the two driving me weren't in the mood for much conversation, but they did want to tell me one thing.

'You looking fucking hideous.'

'So sue me for copyright infringement,' I shot back. 'You've got a case.'

They shut up for a bit. We were heading into town, which meant the station.

In Brighton the town planners put the Police Station, Law Courts, and Job Centre all next door to each other. That tells you everything, doesn't it. Even town planners, famously the most gormless of idiots, can see the connection between joblessness and crime. You can walk from the Job Centre to the Police Station, to the Law Courts, then into a van to Lewes Prison. Do your sentence. Back to the Job Centre, and the cycle starts again.

'Are the handcuffs really necessary?' I asked.

'No,' one of them replied wittily.

'That's just your thing is it?'

'Shut up, Grabarz.'

'Hey, I'm not judging, I like the kinky stuff too. I'd just rather you asked permission first.'

'You better shut up before we pull the car over.'

'And do what? *Not* take me to the police station? I'm shaking with terror.'

'Maybe a bit more than that,' the other one added.

'Then we should probably decide on a safe word.'

'Shut your fucking mouth, Grabarz, or—'

'Or what?' I interrupted, 'Because I don't think you'll do anything. Smack me about and I can walk any charges your boss wants to bring against me. And her boss is just itching to send officers packing, you don't even need to give them a reason. So go ahead, do me a favour.' I waited a moment but they didn't say anything, so I continued, 'In fact, I think I can say whatever the fuck I want.' So I did, 'Your mum likes the kinky stuff too by the way.'

'Don't you dare, Grabarz.'

'And your dad.'

The second one piped up again. 'Can't smack you around, huh? With a face looking like that, who'd be able to tell?'

'People,' I replied. 'People would be able to tell. They're smarter than your species.'

At the station I was quickly corralled into a bright, white room, pushed into a chair, and left alone. Fluorescents hummed above me, stabbing my tired eyes.

Slowly, my eyes adjusted and I could look around. There wasn't much to see. The chairs and table were nailed down. The walls lightly padded to catch some of the screams. On them were advice posters about sexual disease clinics and how to report a crime. I made a mental note to wash my hands afterwards.

There was a recording device built into the table, and a camera in the corner, facing me. Looking down at me with a supervisory and stern expression in its bulbous glass cover. A little red LED sent scum like me the unmistakeable message: YOU ARE BEING WATCHED. I was getting used to the idea.

After what I assume was a deliberately long time the door opened with a loud clank, and the two burly officers from the car came in and stood behind me. They were the kind of big lunks that spent all their spare time in the gym. They were only good for one thing: to get in the way of punches. They're worn as body armour by the smarter officers.

Price sauntered in and took the seat opposite me. Not turning on the recording. Which meant I wasn't a suspect for anything. Yet. She gave a nod to one of the officers behind and they yanked my hands onto the desk, removing the cuffs in the most aggressive way they could.

She didn't notice, she was busy searching through a plastic tray that contained my effects. One by one she spilled them onto the table for me to pick up and return to my pockets.

'One penknife. One book of matches. One cocktail napkin with a doodle on it. One pen. One pad. One very old-looking mobile phone. And one—' she held up a condom. I shrugged and she chucked it onto the table.

As I finished putting them away she kept hold of the last item. My wallet. She was calmly inspecting the contents, I knew she had already done that. She was making a show of it.

'Interesting selection of business cards.' She was mocking me. 'Spencer French, Heating Engineer. Martin Bentley, IT Installation and Repair. Dan Harman, The Argus Newspaper. You know that entering a building under false pretences can be a crime, don't you?'

'I don't know what you mean.'

'Really?' She had been expecting that response.

'Those are genuine business cards, call them and ask.'

'So the receptionist at the school was lying when she told us you were from the council?'

'She must have been mistaken.'

'And the business card?' She pulled it from her pocket in a sealed plastic bag.

'Must have fallen out of my wallet.'

She didn't respond, she was busy pulling another one out, 'Wow! Dean Craggs, Locksmith.' She smirked, 'I bet that one comes in handy.' Then she ripped it in half, 'Oops,' and threw the wallet and cards onto the table.

I pocketed it and scooped up the cards.

'You didn't have any concealed weapons on you. That was lucky.'

It wasn't luck. But I don't need to tell you that. All a private investigator has to do in this country is not get caught doing anything illegal. There are no licences, not like in America. Anyone can set themselves up as a PI and start filming infidelities. That said, everyone in the business knew licences were coming, especially thanks to the phone hacking scandal and public revelations about the dark arts of journalism. In London being a PI can be lucrative if you get in with a tabloid. Break in here. Hack a dead girl's voicemail there. Steal some files, some emails. Just don't get caught.

'We still have you for breaking into the flat.'

I didn't say anything, but she studied me, and maybe she saw something I didn't mean to give away.

'Except we don't,' she was stopping and starting, working things out and making each logical leap as she spoke, 'The sister, she had a key and she gave it to you. Which you didn't tell me last time I accused you because you knew I'd take it off you. Which means you wanted to revisit the flat. Which means you already have.' She nodded to herself, then smiled wryly, 'Find anything interesting?'

I was a little impressed, but I didn't show it.

'Not even a shrine to you?' she added, and slammed one of the photos onto the desk. It was me and Rory at secondary school.

'Exactly what kind of relationship did you have with Rory?'

'We were just friends.'

'And his sister?'

'Even less.'

She took a second to think before continuing, 'Here's how I see things happening: your friend, one of Robert Coward's low-level soldiers, steals a ton of starz from Coward's men and they kill him for it. How does that sound to you?' Half her voice was accusing me, the other half actually wanted to know.

'If he stole them then why were they still in his flat?' I said.

'Because he never told them where they were.'

'So he died to protect some pills?'

'Maybe he died to protect you. Maybe the two of you were in this together.' I could see her thinking, but it was year-one detective thinking. Not the kind of thinking that gets you to DCI at her age.

I leant back in my chair and broke out my wicked smile.

'You're Pistol Penny, aren't you?'

'What?' She was uncomfortable, shifting in her seat.

'As a hard-working taxpayer,' I continued, 'I would just like to thank you for saving us all that money that their fair trial would have cost.' I turned to the two brutes, 'What about you guys? You like the shoot first, lie to review boards later approach.'

'Shut your mouth, Grabarz!' one of them barked, squaring up to hit me.

'Guys! Step outside.'

They backed off instantly, throwing me dirty looks as they shut the door behind them. When I turned back, Price was glaring at me.

'What are you doing?'

I shrugged in a way that would be charming to any other woman. 'I don't trust them.'

'Thanks for the compliment,' she said with no feeling.

'Penny isn't even your real name, is it? Your warrant card says Noël.'

'Penny is my middle name. The newspapers thought it scanned better.'

'P.P.' I sounded it out loud, 'Penny Price. It makes you sound like a superhero.'

She snorted derisively, 'It makes me sound like a superhero's girlfriend.'

It was her turn to lean back in her chair now, relaxed for a moment.

Her suit was sharp and her shirt was buttoned up to the top, just like her, but her blond hair was slightly loose, and I could see that it was naturally curly. I jumped over the desk and pulled off her hair band. Her hair exploded out in every direction in all its big curly glory. It was over her face. Then she flicked it back with a swing of her neck like Rita Hayworth, 'Me?' and we were all over each other. Doing it on the desk. Who cared if the camera was watching, it was a treat for it.

In reality, none of that happened. Just in my mind. She'd probably break my arm, but maybe it would still be worth it.

If only things could have stayed like this between us. But, with a sigh, she refocussed.

'You failed to report an assault on Rory's sister. Who were they?'

'I don't know.'

Once again, she was right behind me. The neighbours had reported it, I guessed.

'Fine, spend an hour with a sketch artist.'

'My memory of the thing is pretty hazy.'

'Spend the whole day with them then.' She wasn't letting it go.

I took a moment to look at her. Top to bottom.

What did I know about her? She had risen through the ranks. She had killed at least six men. Brought down here because she was a good detective, but so far I hadn't seen the evidence. She wasn't corrupt. But she was bendable. She didn't always follow the rules: you don't kill six men by following the rules. And even if she was honourable in her police work, she hadn't been honourable with me. I couldn't read her, she was too unpredictable, too difficult to get a hold of. She was as slippery as wet soap.

'We made a deal that you had no intention of honouring,' I said, referring to the blood work she owed me.

'And you've told me about as many lies as you have truths.'

Fair enough.

She stood up suddenly. I didn't know why she was standing so close to me at first, but when she pulled a sealed envelope from her inside pocket I realised she was positioning herself between us and the camera. We were in the blind spot.

'I'll give you the blood work.' I tried not to look surprised, 'You give me one hour with the sketch artist. And you do the best fucking job you can with them. Don't screw me over.' She placed the envelope on the table.

Well, well, well. Things were so mixed up I couldn't work out if I was wrong about her or right about her. I moved for the envelope but she placed a single finger on it.

'How did you identify him on the beach?'

'I'm afraid that's no longer part of the deal. How did *you* identify him, anyway, you were only minutes behind me.'

We looked at each other, suddenly it seemed so childish what we were doing. I decided to show faith in her for once. That would confuse her.

'He had pectus excavatum. The chest curves in. What about you?'

'Oh, that was easy,' she gave a wicked smile not too dissimilar to my own, 'I had one of my men follow you.'

Jesus Christ. How many fucking people were spying on me? Whoever he was, he was good. At least, I hoped he was.

I did like her, I decided. She was a bit like me, yet nothing like me. I went to say something but I was cut off when an older man in a pressed, starched uniform burst into the room.

'Chief Superintendent!' Price jumped out of her seat.

He didn't look like he would have the strength to open the door. He was grey skinned, grey haired, with tiny wire-rimmed glasses. Dry lips. Sunken eyes. All the appearance of a corpse. And yet he was always upright, as though he had a scaffold pole down his back.

The way he had opened the door we might have been kids having a cheeky snog-session in a cupboard.

She looked to the envelope, but it was already in my pocket.

'Sergeant Price,' he spoke in a weary but unmistakably private-schooled accent, 'I sought you out for this position in order to drag this service's reputation out of the dirt. And then I hear of you consulting with the dirtiest of them all.'

'Always a pleasure, Roy.' I jabbed. He didn't even look at me.

This was the man who had blacklisted me. A paragon of incorruptibility, we were encouraged to believe. Dixon of Dock Green. As stiff and straight as his uniform.

I was trying to leave but he was blocking the door.

'Mr Grabarz witnessed an assault that I believe is connected to our murder.' She sounded afraid of him. Just getting caught in the same room as me was enough to make her feel dirty. 'He's about to sit with a sketch artist.'

The Chief regarded me for the first time in months. He wasn't regarding me as a person, more like the contents of his handkerchief. 'That sounds unusually cooperative of Mr Grabarz.' He turned his gaze back to Price. 'I do hope we haven't given him anything in exchange.'

'Nothing but gratitude,' I answered before she had

to lie.

'Good,' he said loudly.

I tapped him on the shoulder. 'I haven't received the gratitude yet.' I was proud of that one.

I had to spend almost two hours with the sketch artist creating pictures of the bear and the weasel. I thought when she said it that it would be some specky geek with a computer making E-FITs. But this was an actual sketch artist. An arty, middle aged woman called Mary, who clearly made her money through a combination of this, teaching, and selling portraits from a market stall.

She liked me. That's why it took so long. She was trying to keep me there all day, and I wasn't entirely sure that some of time she wasn't sketching me.

Eventually I got out of the station. If I was going back to the school to get whatever was hidden in the den then I needed to make sure I wasn't being followed. I did the usual dry-cleaning. In shops and out the back exit. Dropping things and picking them up. I was alone, whoever Price's man was she hadn't been able to give him the order in time. Either that, or she was leaving me alone now.

To torture myself I decided to walk through the Open Market, almost drowning in saliva at all the things I couldn't afford to eat. Maybe I could survive on the smells alone. Isn't that what supermodels do?

I walked from there to the school through damp air. Storm Joseph wasn't finished, apparently it was giving us a day off today, but it would be twice as bad tomorrow.

I marched past the reception, mud half up my legs, 'Me again,' I looked like a crazy person. Again the receptionist was calling for me to sign in, but I was long gone. Into the woods. Through the wreckage of the den. Price's bastards had been thorough, after tomorrow you wouldn't know the den had ever been here. I knelt down to the tree stump, down to the cavity, and reached inside.

A moment later I was interrupted by more rustling sounds from the trees. *Not Price again!?* It wasn't, it was the receptionist and a balding, vaguely pathetic looking man.

'What the hell is going on here?' the man bleated.

'Who are you?' I asked.

'I'm the head, who are you?'

'Then you're just the man I need to speak to. I'll be sending you a letter in the next few days: there's groundwater from your field rising up into people's homes.'

He went white. I handed him a long stick.

'Jab it in the ground and see for yourself.'

'We don't control the water, Mr Burke.'

'Take it up with our lawyers.'

'Oh, they'll be hearing from me. They'll be hearing from everyone.'

'Glad to hear it,' I said, as I passed him Grimace's card.

I marched away and couldn't help chuckling as I heard him prodding at the mud.

Afterwards I walked to my flat, up my stairs, and fought with my door to get in. I was tired again now. Those two hours of sleep had been used up, I needed more.

Thalia was sitting on the window sill, smoking her last cigarette, wearing one of my shirts and nothing else. It struck me that taking her from her place without packing a bag had left her perpetually naked and unable to leave my flat. This was not something I was going to complain about. Oh, and those curves I mentioned earlier? I was glad to see they were all real. The fact that she was just a little larger than the average woman meant that whatever you liked about a woman, she had plenty of.

'Did you find anything?' was all she asked. I had been gone all day.

I held it up: an ordinary-looking writing pad in a plastic bag. The type with a robust hardboard binding. For university or business notetaking.

Together we pored through the pages. Columns. Two with letters, two with numbers, then a date. Once we had been through every page, Thalia spoke.

'Initials. Initials. Number. Number. Date. Every page the same. What is it?'

I wasn't listening. As I stared at that sharp, un-joined-up writing that I had copied so many times, I could see those last ten years that Rory had lived revealing themselves in front of me, and suddenly, I understood everything.

11

The Last Years of Innocence

RORY STOOD STARING into nothingness. There was dim light making it through the grimy windows, as the sun set over the houses on the other side of the street. This alien room was strangely quiet, he could hear children playing out in the street. How could there still be children in this city? How was that possible? It sounded like they were playing football. They were enjoying their last years of innocence. His last memory of innocence had just dropped dead.

What was in front of him wasn't there anymore, just a vodka haze. His brain had seen it, processed it, then shut it out.

He stood over the body of a young girl, just as I had stood over the body of Jo Whiting, and his brain said no. Just no. No more.

Dealing drugs by night had left him pale. Taking

drugs by day had left him aged. Every sinew in his body overused. His muscles tough like overcooked beef. The sound of a train caught on the wind. He would give anything to be on that train right now.

Ten years ago he was selling baggies of weed on the street. Indulging in plenty of the stuff himself, too. No harm in that. Then from a desperate single room, the type he was standing in now. Making more than any of the shitty minimum wage jobs everyone else his age had.

Drug dealers are bad friends, and as his old friends gave up on him, he made new friends, and now everyone he knew was a criminal or lowlife.

Caught in a strong current, like all the others, he moved on to coke. He got to know the dealers, and being a likable bloke, and being able to count, was soon one of them. Like all of them he skimmed a little for his own use. No harm in that.

At least that way he was out of the streets. It was posh idiots who bought coke. Middle class people. Londoners down clubbing for the weekend, and businessmen, lawyers, PR types, the type of people who think they have it all sussed out. They know what life is about. Anyone who thought they were god's gift to whoever they thought they were god's gift to. It wasn't a real weekend in Brighton to them without some drugs thrown in.

And Rory and his like, they could make even more

money, these idiots didn't know what they were cutting it with, how diluted the stuff was. And when he spent too much one month on gambling or drinking, he could cut it down from fifty-percent pure to forty-five, and write off his debts. No harm in that. But then soon it was thirty-five, then twenty. And people don't want to pay much for eighty-percent veterinary painkillers and who-knows-what-else.

So you come up with a gimmick. He started making his wraps out of lottery tickets and scratchcards. That was Rory's smart streak. Not only were you getting coke but a shot at being a millionaire. It was enough to make his awful product worth it.

But soon he was spending more and more on gambling and booze. It didn't matter how much he was making, he always spent more. So then the purity dropped to less than ten percent and suddenly people aren't buying anymore. I mean, in Brighton it's a buyer's market.

So then profits went down again, and he had to beg more and more from his suppliers. He got in deeper and deeper, racking up bigger and bigger debts. Until he was sitting in his rotten one-room, trying to shut out the sound of the girl through the wall that was fucking to pay for her fix. And he could hear those kids again. But this time they were crying. They were her kids, in the other room, through the other wall. They wouldn't be kids for long. He would drown it out with the radio or the television if the bailiffs hadn't taken them. He would listen to music but all he had was a burner phone. He needed to get out of here. Out of this life. But how do you do that?

'We're all in our own private traps,' someone told him, 'and no one can pry them open from the inside.'

That's when that someone asked him if he wanted to push a legal high. Perfectly legal. And all you have to do is hang out in clubs slipping bags into pockets.

I'd been to the clubs myself. After I first found that packet of starz in Jo Whiting's room I wanted to see how ubiquitous they were. I trawled every club on West Street, and in every one I found the sweaty man in the corner, looking around for undercover police.

I would shuffle up. 'What are you selling?'

They would give me a sideways look. I'm not a clubber, and I refuse to dance just to look like one.

'Don't know what you're talking about, mate.'

'Drugs.' I would say, staring right at them. 'What are you selling?'

'What? I don't know what you're talking about,' they would pretend.

'Drugs!' I would shout as loud as I could. Pretending to think they couldn't hear me.

This would then go one of two ways. The first way they would tell me to keep my voice down and we would retreat to an even darker corner where he would offer me ecstasy, or something better. It was basically 'super-ecstasy', he would say. Kicks in quickly, and the comedown is gentle. No crashing.

'Normally I sell them for twenty quid a bag,' a bag of five, that is, 'but since I can tell this is your first time, you can have it for fifteen.'

I'd tell him I would think about it. 'I might come back later.' Just like you do in a shop.

If it didn't go this way then they would deny they had a clue what I was talking about, and then they would head quickly for the toilets to flush their stuff. They never kept much on them and would re-up regularly, that way if caught they could pretend it was for personal use. I would follow them into the cubicle and shove their head down the toilet whilst I went through their pockets. I would always find starz. The drug problem was more like an epidemic. And a monopoly, considering starz were only coming from one source. Then I would flush it for them. Any one of them could have been Rory, but fate hadn't lined us up yet.

And yet for him it was more than just a better job. Much more than that, the person would tell him. You'll be fixed up with a flat. A posh new-build. They'll even pay for a cleaner. This could be an opportunity to turn your life around.

So how did that lead to this? Standing over the body of a young woman. Surrounded by blood and vomit. Picking up the pills she didn't take, because she didn't need them anymore. They were killing people.

It had to stop. But how? Nothing illegal was happening. *Perfectly legal.*

That only left one option. Put them away for pushing the stuff that *was* illegal. Weed and coke. Plus the ecstasy. Ketamine. Heroin. Whatever pies they had their fingers in.

He walked back to his posh new-build, on the top floor. Pale white. Empty. He could never bring himself to fill it. He had traded one trap for a posher, more modern, minimalist, open-plan trap. He had to get out of here too. But if he went to the police, and if they cared, it would be a long operation. Huge. They would start surveillance and take their good time gathering evidence. And he would have to testify, the trial would take months. He would be dead within a week.

No, the police could only be involved at the very end. The day they arrested them. The day Rory disappeared for good. He would have to bring the noose to them. A complete case. Open and shut. Water tight. Then mum and Thalia would have to disappear too. He would be putting every friend he had in danger. Good thing he didn't have any.

Until then, he couldn't go to the police. Who *could* he go to? He used to know a private detective. A good one. One who worked with the police sometimes. But he hadn't seen him for ten years. He probably wouldn't even take his call. No, he was going to have to do this himself.

Evidence was needed, so he bought a notebook, the robust hardback type used for important work. And in it he recorded every sale. The little ones in clubs, and the big wholesale stuff. He would memorise it through the night, jot it down in the morning. And soon it wasn't just the pills. It was the weed, coke, ket, E's, and smack. He was rising through the ranks, becoming Coward's protégé, getting his eyes into every deal. And getting every deal into his notebook.

He was dedicated. Cleaning himself up. Not using. Getting to know his sister again. Doing everything right that he had done wrong. He was being a detective, and how do you learn how to do that? You need a role model.

So he followed me, taking photos, learning my trade, learning some of my methods. And probably my bad habits too. Redeeming himself in my eyes until he thought I would take him seriously. I would have to be involved eventually. Who better to take the evidence to the police, to negotiate his way out of there. Maybe he wouldn't have to disappear after all? He would turn up at my office. Clean shaven. Hair in a neat ponytail. And present me with a notebook full of evidence. Everything he had done wrong would be forgiven. I would embrace the best friend I had lost. The good man I always knew was still inside. And things would be like they were supposed to have been. Grabarz & Sweet, taking down the bad guys together.

Things never got that far. Rory wasn't a detective. Just a good person who had made bad choices, trying to make them right. He had tried to be covert, but all his behaviour had changed, cleaning himself up at the same time he was getting more involved than ever. These people will kill you just for thinking of going to the police. Just for having a friend or a brother in the police. Just for talking to them. You get arrested, get interviewed for too many hours, and they'll kill you just to be sure. Some officers played this game themselves with the younger ones. Bring them in, buy them a burger, and parade them out the front door with a pat on the back and a smile. Dead by close of play. They even called it the "last meal".

Someone in Coward's crew had got suspicious of something and that was enough. Rory hid the notebook. And just in time. I couldn't help wondering what he thought when they kicked down his door. Did he know he was going to die? Did he think it was all a waste? Did he pray they wouldn't kill Thalia? Did he beg them not to?

It was at this point that I realised I was crying into my drink. It was night now. I had got out of bed and gone to the sofa in the other room. I had ignored Thalia crying the night before, I couldn't lie next to her and start blubbing. It was too embarrassing.

'Can't sleep?'

I jumped. She was in the doorway, in nothing but one of my tops, as always. She didn't even have any underwear anymore.

'I was dreaming,' was about all I could manage.

'Bad dream?'

'About your brother.'

She flicked on the bedroom light, which threw enough onto me to reveal my bloodshot eyes.

'So at least part of you cares.'

She turned back into the bedroom but I was up and had her by the arms.

'Thalia!' I was up in her face, 'He was an idiot,' she tried to pull away but I wasn't going to let her, 'He was a pushover. A flake. And a drug dealer.' She was staring deep into my eyes, anger filling her face, 'But he was always my friend.'

The anger melted into tears. The tears ran down to her mouth. And soon that mouth was on mine. I pushed her backwards, down onto the mattress. Kicking away the duvet. All over her.

The sex was quick, each of us using the other to get what we needed. For her it was connection, emotional release, to share pain, that sort of stuff. She cried through a lot of it. For me, it was sex.

Afterwards, I laid there, starting to feel guilty that it didn't mean more to me, but far more occupied with the joy and pain of having my best friend back. He hadn't been dead, he had existed. Now he didn't.

As I stared at shadows dancing across my cracked ceiling I swore a simple oath:

Rory, you wanted this to stop. I will make it stop.

12

A Time to Do Things Properly

I WOKE UP more rested than any time I could remember in the last few months. I knew exactly what I was going to do with my day. I had a plan.

I left Thalia in the land of nod whilst I showered, shaved, and lightly breakfasted on the last of the left-over pizza in the fridge. I had been surviving on two slices a day. Then I dressed in what was clean in the wardrobe and threw on Rory's old coat. She was still asleep when I left.

I jumped on my bike and headed for George's house. Presumably through some lucky inheritance, he could actually afford a house. A *house*. In Brighton. He lived in Patcham, which back in the day when people travelled by stagecoach used to be the last stop before Brighton. The parish church actually dates from the eleventh century, and parts of that old village can still be seen in cute cottages. But most of Patcham is now pure suburbia. Just the northern most tip of a growing Brighton. You can't go any further north because the Downs are in the way. Between them and the sea they were the only two things reigning the city in. The sky isn't even the limit now.

I rode up Surrenden Road through chill air, underneath a threatening swell of cloud that covered every inch of sky like a blanket about to smother the city. It looked like the underside of some huge ocean, with us on the seabed. The bottom feeders. Storm Joseph was shaking his fist at us, but he wasn't going to strike just yet.

Once I had made it over the hill and into Patcham, I pulled up in the driveway of George's mock-Tudor monstrosity. It even had those leaded diamond-paned windows, like he was an Elizabethan or something. Without a wife or kids he always seemed out of place there to me. There was a token gate, and two stone lions guarding it, but they both looked cheap. Just for show. A fake CCTV camera sat above the door. Of course it was fake, there were no wires. Again, just for show. I was pretty sure that if I knocked on the lions I would hear they were hollow inside, just like everything in suburbia.

I rang the doorbell and was treated to a sickening, electronic rendition of *Ode To Joy*. Soon I heard a shuffling sound and the door was ripped open from the inside. It took him two seconds to recognise me.

'You can fuck off,' was his way of welcoming me.

'Your doorbell seems in a much better mood than you, George.'

'Stupid thing came with the house.'

He wiped his nose, then coughed a couple of times without covering his mouth.

'What the hell do you want?'

'I've got something for you.'

'What the fuck do I care?'

I pushed my way in and marched into his living room. It was a chintzy nightmare. Like someone had let off a grenade packed with doilies. I didn't feel like George had made a single design choice in the room. Except maybe the floor made of empty bottles. In front of the television was an arm chair, a side table, an ash tray, and an open bottle of beer. He saw what I was looking at.

'Want one?'

'Coffee, George, for me.'

'Make it yourself.' He sat down in the arm chair.

'Enjoying retirement?'

'How many times are you going to make me say fuck you, Joe?'

I decided to perch on an arm of the sofa. 'What happened?'

'You know what happened.'

'How did it happen, then?'

He frowned at me at first, but every person wronged loves a chance to tell the story. To moan. I was lucky this was going to be the one time, I'm sure his friends had heard it several. That said, he seemed to give it to me in bullet points, the same way he rattled off witness statements or crime scene details.

'The Chief didn't even do it himself,' he started, 'the Super called me into his office, showed me a copy of the email that the Chief had sent to all officers telling them not to consult with any private investigators. That it was a capital offence. Then he asked if I had seen the email. I told him I had. Then he fired me.'

'How did he find out?'

'You were on the front page of the Argus.'

'Only in silhouette.'

'Tough. He recognised you.'

'That's it?'

'That's it. Pressures on them because of the cuts. There's good Sergeants that haven't been promoted because there's no money for DI salaries. But they hired her. As a DCI! For one of her that means they've got to get rid of two of me. I gave him an excuse to get rid of someone, which is exactly what he wanted, thanks to you.'

'Thanks to me?'

'I haven't said this before, have I?' he said with a smile just creeping into sight.

'Said what?'

'You blacklisted yourself, Joe.'

That's not the way I experienced it. 'How exactly did I do that?' I asked.

'You did something stupid. And nobody made you do it.'

'That kind of depends how you look at it.'

'You can't get away with everything. You should've learnt that by now.'

I looked around again at the dump this nice house had become, 'Hey, I'm still in business, aren't I?'

He picked up his beer and downed it in one long set of gulps, never breaking eye contact with me. Then he dropped it on the floor.

'You're not my friend, Joe. What are you doing here?'

I threw the notebook in his lap. He had to catch it. That should have given him some adrenaline to wake him out of his stupor. He peeled open the pages, not sure what he was going to find, and not sure what it was once he had.

'What the hell is it?' he asked.

'Dealer. Buyer. Amount. Price. Date. A record of every deal Coward's men have done over the last few months.'

When he heard this he shut the book. As though it was something serious that he shouldn't be looking at. 'What do you want me to do with it?'

'You're still a policeman, aren't you?'

'Is that a joke?'

'Get your job back. This is exactly the sort of thing they brought her in to do and you've done it yourself. It's the best Christmas present you or them have ever had. It could do real damage to Coward, maybe even to Max.'

'Not that rubbish again.'

He needed more convincing, so I continued, 'I'm sorry, ok? I do try and do the right thing occasionally.'

He nodded to himself a few times, and then a moment later he stood up. I almost took a step back, I didn't know what he was thinking. But to my surprise he reached out a hand for me to shake. Which I did. But I didn't let go.

'Just do me one last favour.' He tried to pull his hand away but I held on to it, 'Wait till tomorrow.'

He frowned.

'That's all.' I smiled.

We said a few more words. And I left. Now the plan was in motion, it was time to keep going.

I roared back over the hill until I could smell the sea, coasting downhill until I hit the centre and my office. My mouth was already salivating with the thought of all the avocado toast and street food I could afford with the money that was finally coming my way. Just the ability to see something that costs a couple of quid and be able to buy it without an existential crisis should not be underestimated.

I parked up, and round the corner found Lenny in his usual spot. He was wearing his ushanka with the ear flaps down, and his camo coat. He was dressed to fight Storm Joseph.

'Good day, Lenny?' I asked.

'Good day, chief,' he answered in the affirmative.

I loved how someone in such dire straits could always be in a better mood than me. Than most people really. If that doesn't teach you to just cheer the fuck up, I don't know what will.

'Anyone try my door this morning?'

'No one yet.'

I squatted down next to him, avoiding sitting down as I didn't want to get a wet arse.

'Now,' I said, in a probably too patronising tone, 'are you planning to go to the shelter tonight?'

'I always plan to go to the shelter, boss.'

'That doesn't really answer my question, Lenny.'

Someone passing chucked a pound coin in his general direction, it rolled to a stop in front of us. He nodded towards it, as though I was welcome to it.

'I can't take money off you. I'm not that desperate yet.'

'It's not mine.'

'He was giving it to you.'

'I don't want it.'

'Why not?'

'I'm not a beggar, chief, I just haven't got anywhere to live. When they're not chucking coins at me they're frowning at me. People frown at me sitting around here, but where do they want me to be? The only place they don't frown at me is the shelter, but that's only open at night. They frown at me in the library, they frown at me in Churchill Square, as though I've got somewhere to go but I'm choosing to clutter up the street. It's a job I want from them, not charity.'

I just nodded, what was there to say?

'The storm is going to be twice as bad tonight, you need to be in the shelter.'

He didn't completely ignore it, but he changed the subject to his favourite one.

'Did you know that there's not a single piece of the world that white folk haven't ruined?' This was his way of trying to get me to leave him alone. 'India, Australia, America, Africa, the Middle East-'

It worked. 'Alright, alright, Lenny, I'll leave you alone.'

I stood up, scooping up the pound in the process. 'But I'll be back.'

I unlocked the outside door and jogged up the stairs to my office. Inside I hung Rory's coat on a coat hook rather than throwing it over a chair. Not because it was Rory's, but because there comes a time to do things properly. I threw the phone receiver in the air and caught it before I dialled. I was in that mood. After all, I was calling Monica Todman.

The phone rang for some time on the other end. Finally, the receptionist told me she wasn't in the office. Being a detective, I had already sourced her home number so I called that. This was answered very quickly by a male voice.

'Todman household,' was the utilitarian answer. I pictured an odious butler in full period dress.

'Monica Todman, please.'

'Miss Todman is busy, can I take a message?'

'Tell her it's Joe Grabarz. She'll take my call.'

'She is not to be disturbed, sir.'

'Look,' I said, 'I don't care if she's eating, drinking, or under the covers, she'll take my call. Go get her.'

I could hear him thinking, then I sat on hold for an annoyingly long time. The hold music sounded like a four-piece jazz band trapped in a steel box. Eventually the torture stopped.

'Joseph?'

Just her voice, divorced from her body, her face, style, or her dripping Old Fashioned was enough to make me feel gooey inside.

'Hello, Monica.'

'You've caught me in the bath, Joseph.'

I prayed it was true, and on cue I heard the sounds of water swishing around her thighs.

'Lucky me.'

I pictured her barely concealed behind convenient bubbles. Steam rising. A silly long brush to scrub her back with. I needed to stop.

'You've got news?' she asked.

'Put in an anonymous tip on the building site. The police will find a store of prescription drugs. No doubt they ship them in there before routing them out to other locations to be divided and sold. So some days they'll be there, some days they won't, but if you go in the day after a delivery you're guaranteed to score.'

'What are they?'

'I don't know, the packets were in French.'

'I see.'

There was silence for a moment. All I could hear was the crackle of soap bubbles bursting.

'You've delivered for me, Joseph.'

'So you'll drop the lawsuit?'

'It would be a nice excuse to see you again.' If she was the type of woman to giggle she would have.

I've found the best thing to do with comments like that is to ignore them. It makes them work even harder. 'And you'll pay my fee?'

Water swished, she was adjusting herself. 'Why did the police blacklist you?'

None of your business, I thought.

When I didn't answer she asked, 'Is it personal?'

'Sort of,' was my response.

'I want to know anyway,' was hers.

'I punched the Chief Superintendent.'

'Joseph,' she had a scolding tone.

If it's possible to convey a shrug audibly then I did, 'It was going to happen eventually.'

'You know…' more water swished, 'you can come round and jump in the bath with me if you like.'

I could, you know. I knew her address, I didn't even have to be invited.

'Ask me again another time.' Literally any other time, Monica.

'I'm not used to being turned down.'

'I'm sure you're not.' I changed the subject back, 'Pay my fee.'

There was that space again where a giggle would be, then, 'You must be joking.' And she hung up.

Damn. I hadn't expected that development. One part of me in particular told me I'd enjoy chasing her for money. The rest of me thought it was very inconvenient right now.

But at least that was sorted. I wasn't being sued anymore. There was just one more thing I wanted to be sure of before the evening, so I opened up the blood work that Price had given me.

It was Rory's blood alright, but I already knew that. I was interested in the toxicology report. It was broken down rather simply by the doctor for the simple police officers: "Blood alcohol content: 0.07—No illegal substances found."

That settled it. Rory was clean, and pretty much sober when he died. He had passed my final test. He deserved my help, no doubt. *I will make it stop.*

I slumped in my chair. It was only late afternoon, and I had nothing to do until the evening, so I decided to go walkies.

It was between four and five and the Lanes were still full of people, even if most of the jewellers had started taking things out of the window displays, ready for locking up. Lenny was gone though. Good, he had listened to me after all.

Harry was just coming out the shop where he worked, and spotting him I asked him for a quick drink in The Bath Arms. This was when he told me all about young Bobby, about his father, and all that stuff.

Afterwards, I walked out and down through the Steine. The bells of St. Peters were ringing the changes, which is always a strangely provincial sound to hear in such a bohemian city. But it was nice. Almost quaint.

By halfway up Elm Grove I couldn't hear them anymore. Then I was up at the top, in the shadow of Brighton General Hospital. The central clock tower struck seven as I passed it, but I could barely read it in the gathering darkness. The hospital was once the old workhouse, and the place still gave me the chills. It's grey, stained walls had once contained how many screams? How many desperate people unlucky enough to be born poor in that century? How many people with mental illnesses that were misunderstood? Had any of my relatives been trapped in there? Or born in there? I didn't know. I would never know. I can't, but if you can, check their birth certificates for 250 Elm Grove.

It wasn't Brighton's first workhouse, but certainly it's last. For some years after the First World War it became the Kitchener Indian Hospital, to nurse those unlucky Indian soldiers who had fought to protect our empire. The Hindus and Sikhs who didn't survive were cremated on a funeral pyre on the Sussex Downs. Just north of Patcham you can see the small, domed Chattri monument that marks the spot, sitting serene and solitary in the middle of the hillside. After that the building was back to a workhouse for a decade, then it became the hospital it is today.

I continued up towards the racecourse but took a left along Tenantry Down Road and scrambled over the fence into the allotments above the cemeteries and crematorium. Andy kept an allotment around here and I knew he kept a lawn chair in the little lockup.

I planted it down next to his runner beans, just over the fence from the gravestones in the cemetery. Once, on a whim, I decided to see if I had any family buried here, but there was no Grabarz. If that was even his real name.

Right now I sat and watched the sun set over my favourite view of the city. Admiring the curves where Richmond Road and Roundhill Crescent are carved into the hill through which the railway line cuts a tunnel. You can see as far as Shoreham power station and beyond from here. The only thing ruining this view now was the tower of the i360 viewing platform that was still under construction and currently a title contender for World's Most Pointless Tall Pole.

I had fallen in and out of love with this city so many times. There are a load of things about it that piss me off, especially when people act like the place is perfect. It's not perfect. But every time I see this view I'm reminded of what the city really means to me. It's home.

I had been raised by so many families, passed from one to the other, that it felt as though the city had raised me. It was my mother and my father. And if someone hurt it, it was as though they had slapped my mother across the face. Right now, my mother and father had a drug problem, and I was going to do everything I could to make it better. This was my city. *My* city.

Sitting in the allotment, frost growing on the vegetables, amongst the smell of crisp, damp air, underneath what was going to be a storm, amazingly, I fell asleep.

I dreamt of the time that Elaine came and asked me to find Rory. That offended, disappointed tone, *'I don't have any money, Joe.'* And the look she gave me as she left. Contrary to what she thought of me I didn't just ignore her. I did care. And I dreamt of when I went looking for him.

I used an old school photo to trawl the pubs he used to drink in. Then the ones he didn't. In a complete dive the landlord nodded, and gestured to a table in the corner. There was Rory, sitting alone. He looked up and gave me the smile that he always did. I remembered that smile and I gave the one I always gave back. But he wasn't looking at me. Three men pushed past me: the bear, the weasel, and a third, shorter man. I had found him. He hadn't changed. He didn't want to know me. I didn't want to know him. And I would save his mother from ever meeting *this* Rory. They hugged and joked as I slinked backwards into the darkness.

13

Thick as Thieves

IT WAS PITCH BLACK when I woke, and it took me five seconds to remember where I was and what I was doing. Then the salty night air grabbed me by the throat, and shook me a couple of times before it let go.

When the wind paused for a few moments the night seemed silent and still, but I knew it was an illusion, another huge storm front was set to batter the coast in just a few hours. The beating fist of Storm Joseph, and he wore brass knuckles too.

As I climbed over the fence out of the allotments, and headed down Bear Road toward the Roundhill area, I could feel the wind picking up, like God was gradually turning up the dial, and every house I passed began to draw their curtains, turn up the heating, and turn up the volume on their TVs. Cavemen retreating deeper into their caves.

Through the gyratory and up the other side, the wind became a bully that pushed and shoved you around, so that you couldn't walk in a straight line. It was more like a group of bullies, a bully circle if you know what that is. And if you don't know what that is, it's exactly what it sounds like. More and more people hurried into warm, steamed-up pubs and restaurants. There's never anywhere quite as cosy as a softly lit pub with a drink in your hand, food in your stomach, and a storm outside the window. It's just a shame when you have to leave.

The word was that Coward's men still drank at the Roundhill pub where I had seen them two years ago. Apparently it was quite well known amongst junkies, Lenny had told me. They knew to avoid it if they owed money.

The Roundhill? I remembered it was a dive then and thought it was probably still a dive now. And it was.

From the outside I knew the type of place: a place where fat, balding men came to play pool and darts and drink cheap lager and cheap bitter. This was not somewhere that listed the wine with tasting notes and served lovely organic beef burgers in toasted brioche buns. This place was for men whose jobs were slowly destroying their knees and their backs. Men who were paid cash-in-hand and only reported small change to the taxman. The sort of place that anywhere else would casually ignore the smoking ban, but in Brighton even the tradesmen are starting to vape.

It used to have big glass windows, like a shopfront, that were peculiarly clean, probably the only clean thing in the place, that gave walking past it the feeling of passing a natural history exhibit. 'Here we have three old men playing pool whilst another hacks his guts out onto the carpet.' I always thought they did this to discourage new people from entering the place. But now they had replaced them with frosted windows, I guessed they needed the business.

I pushed my way in through the frosted front door, etched with the word "saloon". Ironically or not, I couldn't tell.

Inside was just as I had feared. It smelt of sweat, smoke, dogs, and possibly even urine. My ears were assaulted by the clack of pool balls on pool balls. People screaming at football on the telly. Gambling machines played irritatingly high-pitched renditions of popular game show themes. And from every corner came that irritating banter-laugh that men do to assert their masculinity, just in case anyone was doubting it.

A few people looked at me, it must have been obvious to them that I wasn't a regular, for starters I wasn't wearing the uniform. Polo shirt, rugby shirt, football shirt, it didn't matter but as long as your top was made for doing sport and your belly meant you couldn't see your shoes then you were one of them. I wasn't one of them, but the place was so noisy that their brief moment of interest wasn't registered by anyone else.

In a corner that was half table, half booth, already with a few empty pint glasses, sat the bear, the weasel, and the short, third man, the only other people in the place under forty-five. I sauntered up to them out of the mob. The place was so packed they didn't even notice me until I spoke.

'It's Toby, isn't it?'

I was speaking to the weasel, but of course they all looked up. I must have been quite a sight, with my bruised face, because I saw the bear mouth, 'Jesus Christ.'

'Remember me?' I asked.

'You broke my nose,' Toby said slowly.

'Yeah, sorry about that. Mind if I take a seat?'

'Yeah, I do a bit.'

I looked between the other two, 'Why don't I buy us all a drink?' and before they could answer I was at the bar.

Two men in front of me were holding a third one by his arms and punching him. I would have done something but the landlord was busy watching and laughing. I couldn't afford to get on his bad side, yet. I also thought the guy being punched was laughing, whatever that meant.

I distracted him long enough to order, 'One lager

and three more of whatever they're having,' as I gestured to the corner.

Normally I don't drink beer anymore but the spirits looked shit and anything fancy might get me lynched.

'Three lagers and one snakebite.'

He pulled a couple of the beers and then made the unholy half and half mix of lager and cider that really marks you out as a chav. He added a dash of blackcurrant at the end. Technically this made it a snakebite and black, but I wasn't about to point out his mistake.

He got the last nonic ready to pull my lager, but then I decided that I didn't give a shit what they thought, I don't live my life like that.

'On second thoughts, make mine a shandy,' I said.

The two men suddenly stopped punching the other one, as though they had heard an usual sound, and all three looked at me with a smarmy grin. It was as though I had turned up in drag.

They loosened their joints, leaning on the bar, doing an impression of relaxation. This was a game for them, a chance to take the piss is what they live for.

God, I hate being a man sometimes. We're such a pathetic, posturing, insecure sex. It's irritating when women say "he's only a man, dear" or "they're men" as an explanation, not only because it assumes all men are like that, but because it's giving them an excuse. It's saying "they're men: they can't help it". I'm a man, and I can tell you right now: they can help it.

'You know this isn't Revenge, right?' the leader of the pack asked. Revenge is *the* gay club in Brighton, if you didn't know.

'You're right,' I said, 'Revenge has women.'

'What are you saying?'

'Nothing, it's just a bit of a penis festival in here.'

'Yeah, well you're the one drinking the shandy.'

'Yes, I am,' I replied. 'And you're the homophobe who won't shut up.'

The landlord used the brief silence that followed to ask, 'Was it lager or bitter you wanted?'

'Bitter,' I answered.

He dutifully poured me a bitter shandy, lemonade in first, which is correct.

I had managed to scrabble together my last fifteen quid, which with the pound from Lenny was only just enough thanks to Brighton prices, and picked up the four pints.

'Enjoy your shandy, princess,' the wise guy shouted as I moved away.

'I will, sexy,' I shouted so that everyone who wanted to could hear me, 'I'll meet you in the alley later, and don't forget to pay me this time. This hot piece of ass isn't yours for free.'

Even with him behind me I could feel the heat of him turning as red as an embarrassed homophobic idiot. Amazingly there are still even areas of Brighton that civilisation hasn't reached yet.

When I returned to the corner they seemed to not have heard this exchange, they were too busy talking quickly in hushed tones, which stopped suddenly. I was glad they were talking about me.

'Cheers,' I said as I plonked down the drinks.

'Cheers,' the bear replied.

The short man just nodded his thanks and Toby didn't thank me at all. He really was hairy all over, and bony. Really bony. He looked like he could cut me with his elbows. We all took a sip except him. His was the snakebite.

'So, do you remember me?' I asked him.

He raised his eyebrows and bobbed his head in an irritating way, trying to make me anticipate his answer. Much like the men at the bar, setting up what they think is a hilarious joke.

Then finally, 'Yes,' he replied, 'I said. Of course I remember you, I've got a big painful reminder in the middle of my face.' He paused for breath. 'Why? You want to go again? I'll go again. You got me off guard.' He glared at me. Then, he shouted, 'Yes, I fucking remember you!'

'He means from school,' the short man said.

He had a smooth, prematurely bald head and arms that didn't seem to add anything to his width. He looked like a bullet standing on its end. And yet he was very calm, and came across altogether more thoughtful than the other two. That is to say, he came across as though he had thoughts.

'School?' Toby looked at the others.

This fact had surfaced from down in my memory sometime in the last two days. Now, I'll admit that this is something I could have told you earlier. But where's the fun in that?

'We went to school together?' he asked me.

'Yeah, you don't remember?' I replied.

'No, I don't remember.'

'You were the kid who kept getting nosebleeds. Did that ever stop?'

He looked like I'd reached out and punched him again.

'No it didn't ever fucking stop, but I'm sure you've really fucking helped by breaking my nose in two places,' he fumed. 'Which kid were you? Oh, that's right, no one remembers!'

'I remember you,' the short man said. Then after a pause, 'Joe.'

'Joe?' Toby spoke before I could, 'I don't remember you.'

'You hung around with Rory,' the short man added.

I saw a quick look pass between Toby and the bear, but I had to see it out of the corner of my eye as the short man was keeping his eyes on me.

'That's right,' I said.

'Wait,' the bear seemed to have had an epiphany, 'did you two used to hang out in the trees together like a couple of poofs?'

'Yeah, that was us.'

'I remember you!' he said ecstatically. 'Or at least I remember Rory had a friend.'

'Just one,' I said.

'You guys had a fort in there, that you built in the trees.'

'You remember.'

'Didn't we trash it?'

'Yeah, we rebuilt it.'

'And we trashed it again.'

I swallowed just a mouthful of my pride, 'That's right,' and everyone took a sip of their drinks. Even Toby touched his snakebite.

'So were you gay?' the bear continued, 'I mean, we always thought you were. Would be interesting to know if we were right.'

'None of your business,' I replied.

'That means yes!' he bellowed. Guffawing too. Then he sat back into a reverie, 'Rory's friend...' he took a few more moments to remember the least flattering details he could, 'You were a skinny little kid, weren't you? Quite small.'

I nodded. I couldn't deny it.

'Grubby too. Kind of dirty.'

'Usually. Although I didn't always start that way.'

I took him in from top to bottom. He had blond hair so short that it was practically stubble, and showed up that weird bunch of skin that some bald men get on the back of their head. He looked comical on the tiny pub chair, like he'd be better off with two of them. I was pretty sure he had to book out an entire row if he flew anywhere. But he wasn't fat, he was just large. It was as though he had been made in jumbo, chunky size like a toddler's toy.

'It's Dan, right?' I asked.

'Yeah.' He smirked.

'I remember when Rory won the electronics trophy you stole it.'

'And…?' He was goading me.

'And melted the head with a soldering iron.'

'Yes, I did,' he chuckled.

He was proud. The bastard. You know, most people grow up to regret bullying people. The other people are psychopaths. If I was charitable I'd say he hadn't grown up yet.

'I guess you were jealous.'

'I wasn't jealous!' he shouted. Good, he was insulted.

'Why else would you do it?'

'I don't know!'

'Because that's how school works,' the short man said. As calmly as ever.

'Care to explain that?' I asked.

'It's a Darwinian struggle for superiority.'

Interesting. This seemed to confirm him as the

only one of the three who had ever had a thought that lasted longer than a second. He interested me. He didn't need to speak loudly, or be overly aggressive to assert his power, they knew he was in charge. I knew it too. He was smarter than them. Much smarter. It was to him that I should be speaking.

'What's that measured in?' I asked.

'Popularity, of course.'

He took a sip of his drink, and we all waited for him to explain further. Which he did.

'If it makes you feel better, you fulfilled a very important social function. Each year-group subconsciously selects a few people who are there to be bullied. Usually the weakest or weirdest. And popularity comes from how well you humiliate them.'

He took another sip.

'We all remember them, and we all bullied them, all of us. Some physically, some verbally, some just with cruel jokes to our friends. The "retards". The "spastics". Whatever we called them, they were the piñatas that popularity fell out of when you kicked them.'

'Yeah, I remember!' Toby shattered any interesting thoughts we were having, 'It was you that we put in the bin and rolled down the hill.'

'Yes!' Dan added, intelligently.

'Yeah, that was me!' I pretended to laugh, their smiles broadening. 'I remember when I crawled out, Alan,' I turned to the short man, 'you kicked me so hard it dislocated my jaw.'

I stopped laughing. We all stopped. Smiles too.

'Are you still in touch with Rory?' Alan asked.

'No. We sort of drifted apart.'

'It happens.'

'Not to you guys,' I said, 'You were as thick as thieves then, and look at you now: still thick and still thieves.'

'Excuse me?' Toby said. He seemed not to have got it.

Dan had, 'Sorry about your hand,' he said, pointedly.

'Don't mention it,' I reassured him.

'Still hurt?'

'A bit,' I replied, 'What about your balls, still hurt?'

He wasn't amused. I turned to Toby.

'Look, I really am sorry about your nose. I wouldn't have done it if your friend didn't have his hands around my good friend's sister's throat.'

'That wasn't what it looked like,' Dan lied.

'Oh really? So you weren't shaking her down to try and find Rory's notebook?'

They all fell silent. Each of them stared at me. I just smiled.

'What fucking notebook?' Toby sounded genuine.

'Or were you looking for your big bag of pills?'

'Where's the notebook?' Alan asked quietly.

'Where are the pills!?' Toby pretty much shouted.

'With the police, I'm afraid.'

'Where's the notebook?' Alan asked again.

'I want to see Bobby.'

Toby pretended to chuckle. 'Who's Bobby?'

I put on my most patronising tone, 'Your boss, Toby, you remember him?'

'Hey—'

I interrupted him, 'Taking me to Bobby is the only thing that's going to keep you out of jail.'

Dan and Toby stood up, knocking their chairs over in the process.

The pub froze. Silent. But Alan stopped the other two.

'Sure thing,' was all he said. And he gestured, *after you...*

14

Storm Joseph

THEY LED ME to the back seat of a black 4x4 where they left me for a while. It was plush and warm, an expensive German model with leather seats that felt like they were spooning you.

Blown into the street, tin cans and empty bottles were careening down the hill, spilling into the main road, the now departed residents of recycling boxes. The lids of these boxes slid down the road too, like tea trays. The road's one tree bent and bowed, and the street lamps were dancing a merry waltz.

Alan, Dan, and Toby were standing windswept on the pavement a few metres away, I could see them throwing an argument between them like a cricket ball. Then Alan pointed to the car and they came and sat with me.

Toby was silent in the passenger seat, and Dan was

silent next to me, taking up both the right hand and middle seats. Alan was now on the phone. The conversation didn't seem to be a happy one, his face was one big frown and he was nodding, taking his orders no doubt. I asked the other two what was going on, but they both ignored me, staring out at the storm.

Eventually Alan joined us, and leant over the back of the driver's seat.

'You're in luck, he wants to see you.'

'I'm honoured,' I said sarcastically. He wasn't amused.

'Put these on,' he ordered, and passed me a pair of blacked-out goggles and ear defenders.

There was no point in arguing if I wanted to make it to the meet, so I did as I was told. Once I was kitted out I felt the vibrations of the engine roaring to life. The idea was that I wouldn't know where we were going, of course. But they had forgotten this was *my* city.

We headed down Ditchling Road all the way to the Steine, then along Edwards Street past the police station, courts, and job centre, then into Kemptown.

Kemptown sits between the centre of Brighton and the marina. It's now seen as an arty area, as it's the sort of place where thirty years ago creative types could afford to buy flats. It was also one of the places that had spare space for social housing, so just like Brighton in general it squashed the rich and the poor into the same neighbourhoods. You could probably also describe it as the real centre of Brighton's gay community, but the need for such a place has slowly died out over the last couple of decades.

It was originally the site of Kemp Town, at one point the largest housing crescent in Britain, a once-beautiful regency estate with large cream houses and mews where the servants lived, completed even after Thomas Read Kemp fled the country to avoid his debts (not being able to afford a house in Brighton has an illustrious pedigree).

Now they're all expensive flats, not that that fact really distinguishes the area. And despite the bohemian reputation Kemptown is still the site of the only private school the city really cares about.

We pulled up down one of the mews and I was manhandled out of the car. For those thirty seconds I was assaulted by the blast from the storm, especially that close to the sea. It was like being marched through a carwash.

When the goggles came off I was sitting in a dark room. A dark, but also shiny room. The lights were off but I recognised fairly quickly that it was a stainless steel restaurant kitchen. I reasoned it must be one of the many independent, and highly regarded, restaurants in the area, presumably a front for laundering Coward's drug money. But it could just as easily be a vanity project, a nice hobby to keep him busy when he's not destroying the city or having people killed.

It looked expensive. There was a clean row of ovens and gas hobs. An island of hot cupboards. A huge bank-vault-sized door to a walk-in fridge, and an identical one into a freezer. Saucepans hung from the ceiling, and running along the far wall was a long magnetic strip. Every variation of chef's knife clung to it. Nothing in this place was soft. Everything was sharp.

I was sitting in a metal chair. Opposite me was another. Empty. They had gone through my pockets and my phone and knuckleduster were on the side, too far out of reach. I couldn't hear any traffic, but it was late, and who the hell was going to be out in this weather?

Alan, Dan, and Toby were standing in the corners of the room. Completely silent, as though we were about to receive royalty. I spotted a proper-looking coffee machine sitting on the side.

'Could I get a cappuccino?'

They didn't even look at me. Instead, Alan nervously checked his watch.

Thunder rumbled all around us, shaking the cabinets. Rain was beating against the few tiny windows. Storm Joseph was here in full force. I imagined what I could see if the ceiling was made of glass. Good thing I was inside.

A few minutes later I saw a bead of sweat creep from Alan's hair, down over his temple, to his chin, over the moles on his neck.

Toby was swallowing in my left ear, far too often,

and too loudly, gulping gallons of saliva.

Dan was clenching and unclenching his fists. Cracking his knuckles.

Finally, the sweat arrived on Alan's shoe. Then there came the sound of a car pulling up and headlights swept across the room through the small windows at the top of the back wall.

A car door opened and closed. And then the back door to the kitchen opened, the one I assumed I came in by. In stepped a hard-looking young man. He had a stubbled head and a tattoo poking up from under his collar. His face was scarred, and hard, but this image was rendered ridiculous by the full-on, gold-buttoned, Parker-from-Thunderbirds style, chauffeur's uniform he was clearly forced to wear. He disappeared for a moment and another car door opened and shut.

Then in slithered Robert Coward. He was wearing a midnight blue, full length coat. Purple velvet suit jacket, black trousers, and pointed brown shoes with giant buckles. Silver silk scarf, black leather gloves, and a rose in his buttonhole. He could have been stepping out onto a fashionable red carpet, but instead he was here. His face was sharp, his eyes keen, and his tongue darted out of his mouth from time to time, giving him the general appearance of an overdressed reptile.

He took off his coat and handed it, scarf, and gloves, one-by-one to his driver, who shut the door and stepped back into the shadows. Opening that door had brought more than a chill to the room. Or maybe that was just Coward.

Rather than regard anyone in the room, he went and opened the walk-in fridge of all things. From it he emerged with a big stainless steel bowl covered in cling film.

'Antonio makes the best French onion soup,' he said to no one in particular.

His voice was a big baritone. Much bigger, and about twenty years younger, than his octogenarian body. There was some impression of an old stage actor, who had trained his voice to project to the last row of the gods, but with some flavour too of a hard-drinking, hard-living artist, akin to Hemingway or John Huston, but also taking a far more dandyish pride in his appearance than either of those. To be honest, I didn't know exactly what he was, but he was nothing like the thuggish brute I had expected, and nothing like the brat I had imagined in Harry's story.

He poured some of the bowl's contents into a saucepan and lit a gas burner underneath. Everyone just watched. Then he grabbed an empty bowl and a spoon and sat in the chair opposite me.

'Don't let it boil this time,' he grumbled to his driver. Then he looked at me and acknowledged my existence for the first time. 'Do you know what the secret is to great French onion soup?'

I just stared at him, incredulous. Despite it being a

simple question, I had no idea what he wanted from me.

'Do you know?' he asked again, his brilliant white eyebrows dancing along to his words like two conductor's batons.

'No.'

'It's judging the sweet spot.' He smiled, and leant forward as though I gave a shit. 'You have to caramelise the onions to a deep, dark brown. But not burn them.' He emphasised that last point very strongly. 'It takes a great chef because depending on the butter, on the temperature, on the onions, it's always different. You have to know when to stop. But it's difficult, because the longer you cook them the darker they go, and the tastier they get. But then—' he clicked his fingers, 'they're burnt. And all you're making then is bitter-tasting onion water.' He leant back in his chair, very satisfied with his story.

'That's a lovely story,' I reassured him.

'It's going to come back up later in the conversation,' he said without a smile, 'I promise.'

'What makes you think you're in charge of this conversation?'

This time he gave an ophidian smirk. 'Because I'm in charge of everything.'

I tried not to nod. If I did it's because I knew he would say that.

He looked at my bruised face, '*You're* the bastard

who broke into my building site.'

I nodded, smiling slightly.

'I should have guessed that bitch would hire you.'

He put the empty bowl down on the worktop and straightened his back, getting into work mode. He also pulled his shirt cuffs back out the end of his sleeves.

'Joe Grabarz. We've never met, but I know you by reputation of course.'

'Likewise.'

'You wanted to meet me. Something about a note-book. I suggest you start talking.'

'I'll try and cut through the crap,' I started, making sure they were all listening. It felt like a duel. Things were going to happen quickly. 'I'm an old friend of Rory's.'

He did nothing but raise his eyebrows, and only a millimetre.

'Rory Sweet,' I reiterated.

'Yes, I knew who you meant,' he replied calmly.

Normally when you say to a person the name of someone they've ordered killed it registers as some kind of emotion on their face. Anger, guilt, regret, something at least. I was getting nothing.

'A few months ago Rory started keeping a record of every deal you guys made. A very thorough record.'

'In this "notebook".'

'That's right. Enough to put you all away.' I looked specifically at him now, 'Even you.'

He still didn't react. Either he didn't believe me about the notebook, or he didn't believe that it could put him away.

'I can make sure that doesn't happen,' I said.

He leant back in his chair, and briefly inspected his nails. I was sure he had them manicured.

'I see,' he replied. 'You are a businessman, that is your reputation. How much do you want?'

'I'm afraid money doesn't interest me.'

He laughed so suddenly that I was insulted. That laugh wasn't an act, it wasn't under his control. 'Oh, really?' he bellowed. 'I find that hard to believe.'

'That notebook could cause you and your associates a lot of trouble: there's some pretty big names in there.'

'There's no names, Mr Grabarz. Just initials.'

'And how much surveillance do you think it would take to work them out?' I raised my eyebrows, then I dropped my bomb. 'I don't suppose Max will be very pleased about that.'

His face dropped. But where I thought there would be fear, where I had expected to see panic, I saw only disappointment.

Regardless, I continued, 'Tell me who he is and that notebook will never make it to the police.' Sure, maybe I was betraying Rory, but he would understand. He wanted it to stop. If he wanted I could cut the head off this snake, or I could set fire to the whole slithering bunch.

If there is a man behind everything, if there is a puppeteer pulling every string, if there is a devil in my city, his name is Max. The problem being, that's about all I know.

'That's your deal?' Coward asked quietly.

'That's it.'

'That's a shame.' He readjusted. 'I was hoping to keep this suit clean.'

Thunder rumbled, I could feel it through the chair. And he casually pulled *the* notebook from his inside pocket.

I went spinning. Like those times when you stand up too quickly. I was worried I might fall off the chair.

Then he articulated everything I was thinking, better than I ever could.

'Never trust a policeman, Mr Grabarz. Especially not in this town.'

Then he took the saucepan off the hob and placed the notebook there instead. It began to burn and smoke.

George. The same George who told me ABC Construction was clean. George, who took my money freely, so of course he took it from others too. George, who lived in an enormous house in Patcham that he could never afford. Rory had been given a flat, what had George done to earn himself a house? The smoking notebook began to fill my nostrils.

His tongue darted out of the corner of his mouth,

wetting his lips. 'You know, I was actually expecting to pay you tonight, for a job well done.'

What the fuck was he talking about?

'Who do you think ordered George to text you about the body? I knew you were a friend of Rory's, in fact I was ecstatic to find out. I used to enjoy reading about you, Mr Grabarz. You cheer me up. "The police's dirty habit."'

What the *fuck* was he talking about!?

'When it became clear that we weren't going to find the notebook, I decided you would be the best man for the job. Do you really think I'd let a body wash up on the beach? Do you think that little of me? I thought you would be the best man for the job, and you were.'

He paused, giving another disappointed sigh.

'But tonight you've said one word that means you can never leave this place. And I mean *never*. Where did you hear it?'

I didn't answer, I was watching the notebook burn. The one thing Rory had done with his life to make it all worthwhile.

'You can tell me now, or you can tell me later. But you *will* tell me.'

His driver wheeled over a restaurant trolley. Out of the corner of my eyes I saw him pick up an implement.

'I will start by pulling out your teeth.' They were pliers. A flash of white told me he was smiling. 'I got five out of Rory before I realised that wasn't going to be enough.'

He put them down, and picked up something else. My instincts told me they were secateurs. I was busy seeing my best chance to ever stop this evaporating in front of me.

'I chopped off just this little piggy,' he was holding up his right little finger, 'but Rory had been snorting coke for ten years. Along with the drinking. His heart was too weak. The shock killed him,' there came that white again, 'I missed the sweet spot. *See*.' He licked his lips again.

He wanted a reaction, an acknowledgement of how clever he was. I didn't give him one.

'The fact that he was weak saved him a lot of pain. We didn't even move on to the acid.' He replaced the secateurs. 'How is *your* heart, Mr Grabarz?'

Did he want me to be scared? I was too busy watching the best thing my friend had ever done go up in smoke. Because of me.

'My friend died to protect that notebook.' Through torture, and death.

'Yes,' he nodded, 'and you can see now how pointless that decision was. Don't repeat it.'

I could feel the three stooges approaching me from behind. I suddenly became aware again how sharp, and heavy, and hot everything in the room was. They should have tied me down.

'Before we do this,' I raised my hands, 'just tell me,

where did you dump Rory's body?'

He looked to the others.

'The marina,' Alan grunted.

I nodded. 'That's all I really wanted to know.'

He nodded his head angrily at them. They marched on me. Just as they made it within reach a blinding flash of lightning stabbed into our eyes from every steel surface. It was just what I needed.

I ducked backwards, throwing my chair across the room. I was behind them now. I grabbed the back of Toby's head and slammed his face down on the counter top. He screamed and fell to the floor, his nose bleeding everywhere.

Dan swung. I dodged. And I kicked him right in the testicles. He hollered and dropped to his knees. I grabbed the discarded saucepan from the hob, spilling the soup everywhere, and smashed it into his face, burning him in the process. He writhed around on the floor.

Alan approached, but he slipped on the soup and fell down. I kicked him as hard as I could. There was a crack, and he clutched his jaw.

Coward turned around in fear to his driver, 'Lou!' but he had fled. Leaving just a pile of Coward's hilarious clothes in the dirty doorway, which was now open. The door banged against the wall in the storm.

I stepped over the writhing bodies towards him, slipping my phone into my pocket and slipping my knuckleduster onto my fist in the process. I slapped him.

'Don't leave that chair.'

Then I dragged the three idiots into the walk-in freezer and shut the door, knowing there was no handle on the inside.

When I returned Coward was gone. That son of a bitch had lived up to his name. I was by the open door, he couldn't have got out that way, which meant he was still inside. I flicked the light switch. Nothing happened. Storm Joseph had given me the lightning with one hand, and taken away the power with the other.

I headed outside, maybe his car would have something. It was a customized Rolls Royce, my perfect car. Still running, no doubt his driver had been keeping it warm for him. There was a pathetic little torch in the glove compartment. It would have to do.

I ran back into the kitchen, the feeble yellow glow reflecting off the steel. The only thing I could hear was the hiss of the gas burner. I turned it off. The notebook had collapsed into a pile of ash, some of which was floating through the air.

I checked the main restaurant. Crisp, stylish décor. It was empty. The door was locked.

There was an office off the kitchen, all chipped paint and dust. A battered computer. But no Robert Coward.

Air brushed up my trouser legs, caught in a draft.

It was heading for the open door, but coming from below me through the floorboards.

Cellars. The cellars under Kemptown. The same cellars everyone, including little Harry and Bobby, used to retreat to during the Brighton Blitz. Where was the trap door? It had to be in the kitchen.

Less than a minute searching and I found it. It took some strength to open, I wondered how the eighty-odd Coward had managed it. Adrenaline, I guessed.

I stepped down into the darkness, down rickety wooden steps. The first thing I saw was dusty wine bottles racked up. Then more as I moved into the small cellar, seemingly made of cobblestones. There were lights drilled into the ceiling, I tried them but they didn't work either. I didn't expect them to.

The whole room was full of wine, probably what had been in the cellar for a hundred years. Lost to time. I felt lost to time myself. Down here I couldn't hear a thing. No storm, no footsteps.

It was damp and mouldy, the air thicker and heavier than the storm above the surface. Musty, like opening a shut-up house filled with skeletons and cobwebs. And underneath this smell, the smell of something else. Meat, maybe. I needed to hold it together.

There was a stone tunnel connecting off the cellar, I moved into that. My feet smacking on a film of muddy water that ran across the ground. Just occasionally I heard the wind slamming the door upstairs.

Off the tunnel were alcoves, once secured with iron barred doors, giving the impression of some medieval jail. Just my imagination, I was sure.

Inside the cells were stacks and stacks of starz, amongst some other sacks of god-knows-what. This was the distribution point. Shipped into the marina in the concrete trucks, then shipped here in catering trucks. Then split up and sent off. I wondered if the restaurant did deliveries, it would explain the final step.

After three cells on each side, one of which was open, the corridor opened on to another cellar. This one was empty. The ground was soft. Uncomfortably soft. There was no stone, just soil. And the soil looked wet. I could smell something. Something chemical. Did they cut the drugs here?

I heard a hurried breathing. Panicked. I looked to my left. Leaning in the corner, sweating, pale, and manic was Robert Coward, with a gun in my face. It was a small revolver.

'Don't take another step,' he said between breaths.

One of those cells must have contained an arsenal, just in case.

'This is where we make people disappear,' he whispered.

It was lye I could smell. They would dig a shallow

grave down here and then pour lye all around to speed up the decomposition. I wondered how many bodies were underneath my feet. What was seeping into my shoes?

'I'm not going to kill you,' he said, 'but I suggest you get out of here before I change my mind.'

'Why?' I asked, 'I'm nothing special.'

'I'll give you ten seconds.' He cocked the gun.

'Bobby,' I said with a sigh, 'the gun's not loaded.'

'Are you willing to bet your life on that?'

'Yes, I am. You have absolutely no problem with killing me, upstairs you were about to torture me to death. If the gun was loaded, I'd be dead already.'

I moved toward him, he kept it pointed at me but it never went off. I ripped it from his hands and threw it away. Then I dragged him by the collar back through the cellars, and back up to the restaurant.

I threw him down into the metal chair and pulled mine closer to it. He looked at me with real fear this time. Thunder rumbled, everything shook.

The area around the cooker was black with soot, I ran my finger through it.

'My friend died for that notebook. Burning it is the biggest mistake you've ever made.'

I punched him with my brass knuckles, opening up a cut above his eye.

'He wanted me to take you to the police. Now you just get me. How's your heart, Bobby?'

I picked up the pliers. Clamped them over one of his front teeth. He eyes stayed fixed on mine, I couldn't tell what they were trying to say.

'There's only one thing that's going to save you,' I bellowed as I squeezed those pliers as hard as I could, not trying to pull the tooth, but crush that old thing where it was.

'Whatever you do to me,' he managed to say through the pliers, 'he'll do worse.'

I squeezed the pliers harder than I could, shaking with anger. 'Tell me who he is!'

'I can't!'

In that moment, I saw everything in his eyes. He wasn't afraid of me. He wasn't angry at me. He wasn't defiant or stubborn. Those open whites. Those big pupils and arched eyebrows. He was sorry for me. He pitied me! He couldn't tell me, even if part of him wanted to. He had been here before me, tried for his own sake and failed, he understood what I was trying to do and he knew that it was pointless.

I dropped the pliers and dropped to the floor. I was done.

'Don't be disappointed,' he whispered. 'There's just no one like Max.'

Don't say that name! I launched up and grabbed him by the scruff of his neck and dragged him toward the door.

Outside, red lights in my face, I bundled him

through the condensing exhaust fumes into the boot of his Rolls Royce. And slammed it shut.

LAST CHAPTER

Kiss and Tell

THE NEXT MORNING when I arrived at the office there was someone waiting for me. I was only halfway up the stairs when I could already see a silhouette through the rippled glass, sitting at the unused desk, of all places.

The door was unlocked. I could see that from the light making a clean frame around the door. No one else had a key. So it was with some nerves, and one hand in my pocket, that I pushed it open. It swung all the way without resistance, freely on its hinges like it had been oiled. I didn't recognise this door, and I didn't recognise the office in front of me.

The inside had been tidied, varnished, and everything looked clean. No dust to draw pictures in anymore. There was a new pot plant to keep the old one company, and to give it something to strive for. There was an antique hat and coat stand for clients to hang their antique hats and coats on. And against the walls there were button-back leather sofas for them to park their arses on.

Art adorned the walls. Classy art, a print of Edward Hopper's *Nighthawks* taking centre stage. This was an office I would be proud of, I wished it was mine, but it couldn't be. Not with my luck.

The receptionist's desk was uncovered, clean, with a working telephone, a notepad, and a laptop. Sitting at the desk, wearing an enormous smile, looking at me over a pair of stylish, but I knew unnecessary, spectacles was a beautiful young woman in a professional, but not too professional, black dress. It was Thalia.

'Morning,' she chirped.

I didn't know how, but I had to admit she had done an incredible job. By which I mean I had to admit it to myself.

'I can't pay you without clients,' I said.

She held up the notepad. 'That's ok, you've got appointments all afternoon.'

I couldn't help but smile.

'I didn't know what time you'd be in,' she continued, 'I wanted to surprise you.'

'You succeeded.'

She must have pinched my key and copied it. Maybe she would be a good detective herself.

I felt embarrassed just thinking that, as though she might read my mind and find out I was complimenting her. Some women can do that. A lot of them in my experience.

'I had to kick out four homeless guys when I got in, they were sleeping on the steps.'

Bloody hell, Lenny. It was like feeding a stray cat, the next day they brought all their friends. Soon I would end up with my own troop of Baker Street Irregulars. Until today that wouldn't have ruined my image, but now I looked respectable.

'Any messages?' I asked as I headed into my office.

'Price keeps calling.'

'Tell her I'm not in,' I yelled to her as I sat down.

She had even tidied in here. The blinds had been dusted and my drawers organised. She had even wiped the dust off the bottle in the third one down. I swear my chair didn't squeak anymore.

She had also put the morning edition on my desk. The headline was "LOCAL DRUG RING CRUSHED" and it was apparently a fourteen-page special. Below the fold was "CARNAGE FROM STORM JOSEPH" along with the front page picture: a tree smashed into a car, crushing it like a cricket bat would a tissue box. More pictures were on pages two to five, apparently.

I wasn't interested in that, so I settled in to read what had happened in Brighton over the last few days, according to Jordan Murrows.

Apparently it had all started earlier in the week when that "gruesomely disfigured" body had washed up on the beach. It repeated the details of the disfigurement, much to the joy of the editors I'm sure. Just as the story started to tell you something you didn't already know the front page ran out and you had to buy the damn rag. Continued on page five. This meant I had to flick through three and half pages of people with inside-out umbrellas and pebbles half burying the benches on the seafront. More trees ripped out at the roots, and roofs missing some of their slates. Then the story I wanted to read continued.

Thanks to the work of former Metropolitan Police officer and new Brighton Detective Chief Inspector Penny Price, the body had been identified as Rory Sweet, a local man and known drug dealer. The murder was believed to be connected to organised crime. The article then took its time reminding everyone of the Pistol Penny story.

When it got back on topic it was under the subheading "CACHE OF DRUGS FOUND AT CONSTRUCTION SITE". It detailed a police raid on the construction site in the marina, where a large amount of prescription drugs had been seized due to incorrect and potentially fraudulent import and customs licences. These drugs were believed to be the same "so-called legal highs" responsible for twenty-three deaths over the last few months. Jordan was a little hazy on the connection between Rory's death and these drugs. The article also stated that there were possible grounds to arrest dealers due to European Union regulations on prescription drugs, but that the police would not comment at this time.

It continued, "whereas many have been quick to praise the work of the police, M. Todman, the owner of Todman Concrete who has been fighting a legal battle with those operating the marina construction site commented that the investigation would not have been broken without the help of private investigator Joseph Grabarz. Mr Grabarz said in a statement that he could neither confirm nor deny any involvement in the investigation, but that he considered the comments to be very flattering."

Did I really? Well done, Thalia. I assumed it was Thalia, and not Murrows making things up. But no, I had been rude to him so he wouldn't make up a nice thing like that.

It really was a very good statement, after all, discretion is my business. I never kiss and tell. It would be especially good if it led to more clients like Monica Todman.

The next section was headlined "MASS GRAVE IN KEMPTOWN". This was a peculiar story. It stated that three men had been found injured and locked in a freezer in a Kemptown restaurant. The police had been alerted by an anonymous tip, and later discovered a shallow grave in the cellar that was suspected to contain the heavily decomposed remains of several unidentified persons. This investigation had only just begun and no doubt this story was going to run and run. I wouldn't get to read about anything else for months.

Also in the cellar were more of the same prescription drugs, and a store of illegal firearms. And as if this wasn't coincidental enough, the men matched the description of three men who committed an assault on a young woman in the Moulsecoomb area earlier this week. That was wrong of course, it was Bevendean.

The men were known to be involved in criminal activities, and although they had not yet commented on the circumstances of their chilly incarceration, sources close to the investigation believed that it was the result of a conflict between rival criminal organisations. The words "gang warfare" were used with barely disguised glee.

Finally, the fourteen-page special ended with a section titled "BUSINESS MAGNATE MISSING", explaining that a joint-owner of the construction company, whom police were interested in speaking to, had disappeared. More sources close to the investigation believed that he may have fled the country to avoid prosecution.

And that was the end of it for today. TV listings

next. Then what was on stage, then puzzles, classi-
fieds, estate agent listings, restaurant vouchers, and
sport.

All in all, I thought it had been a hell of a week for
Brighton, and probably no one had noticed. With ink
on my hands I folded up the paper and placed it in the
bin where it belonged.

I slumped back in my chair, opened the third
drawer down and fingered that brandy bottle. I wasn't
going to drink any, I just liked the feel of it.

What had I achieved? Well, the drug problem was
gone. Until the next new drug arrived. Rory's killers
were going to jail, but I had no idea for how long, and
quite what for. The notebook had been destroyed, so
any hope of taking down the whole network had van-
ished. Someone would inherit it. Andy would have to
change the names on his wall. And Robert Coward…
well, I didn't want to think about that.

I hadn't made any progress on Max. But a week ago
I didn't think I was going to, and week later I hadn't,
so who cared. I'd get him one day. At the very least I
had restored Rory's reputation in the minds of the only
three people who cared about him. I still couldn't look
Elaine in the eye, and I wasn't looking forward to the
funeral. But I had made him a nice memory, one to be
enjoyed, not avoided. That was the real victory.

I spent the afternoon meeting the clients Thalia
had lined up. They were a reliable, if not particularly

diverting bunch of losers. They would pay the rent. I managed to get fifteen percent retainers out of three of them, which was more than enough for a trip to the cinema and dinner at Browns. The film was about some superhero nobly defending his city. Good on him, I thought.

With the dinner I treated Thalia. Cocktails or coffee, steak or lobster, you name it. It was my way of saying thank you without having to actually say it, and she repaid me by putting me on the spot.

'So what am I, your secretary?' she asked over a liqueur coffee.

'If you want to be.'

'It isn't about what *I* want. What do *you* want me to be?'

I knew what she was asking, so I didn't answer.

'Just your secretary?'

She pushed even further with her eyebrows, and this wasn't a situation where I could run away so I answered her honestly.

'Thalia, I'd love to use you. Have you work for me, do the chores I don't want to do. Then sleep with you, as I want, and feel no obligation to do anything more about it. How does that sound?'

She nodded, not in agreement, just in understanding.

'You know, Joe, you're a good man,' she said, 'just not a nice one.' I thought that was about fair.

I had treated her to dinner and she treated me when we got back to mine. She was sleeping there temporarily until she could find a new place. It had better be temporary I told myself, I couldn't spend my entire life in somewhere as clean as that office, I'm allergic. Although the job normally takes care of that.

Half an hour later, I was shook out of near-sleep by someone banging on the door. I tried to ignore it, hoping whoever the hell it was would give up and go away. They didn't. Instead I might not have to open the door at the rate they were going, they might get through on their own.

I ran some water around my mouth and climbed up off the mattress. When I did open the door it was the last person I wanted to see.

'You know, for a split second I thought we were on the same side,' she shouted into my face.

She looked a bit manic. Tired. Her blonde hair sticking out unkempt. I have that effect on women eventually.

'That was stupid of you,' I growled, my voice still raw. 'What changed your mind?'

'Well I can't exactly put Robert Coward in a jail cell, can I?'

I didn't answer. Legal highs, a mass grave, a missing kingpin, no doubt she had a mess on her hands, and heaven knows what her bosses made of it all. Maybe they didn't make anything of it, maybe they believed whatever they read in the papers. Anyway, I had done my job, now it was her turn. It wasn't my fault she had chosen the one with more paperwork. I felt more sorry for Andy, I had fucked up his pyramid chart.

'I know what you did,' she intoned.

'What's the matter, Detective? You've never broken the rules before?'

'I know what you did.' She repeated it like a robot, the same tone as before.

I looked down the corridor. 'You're alone out there. Doesn't seem like you know much.'

'I know what you did!' she shouted.

I looked her up and down. I have to say I was disappointed.

'Yeah, well, I know what *you* did.'

'I didn't do anything!' she screamed.

'Exactly,' I said. And I shut the door on her.

I drifted back to the mattress, trying to shut out the sound of her continuing to bang away.

'I know what you did, Grabarz! I know what you did!'

It was no good, and against my best efforts I began to think about what I had done.

* * *

I could see myself piloting that enormous car through Kemptown's tiny streets. Through the endless fog. There was not a soul in sight. I could get away with anything.

The wrong way down the Marina Way off ramp, and down the spiralling flyover. Into the ghost town. Towards the construction site. I drove the Rolls Royce right through the fence. Even leaving the lights on as I bundled Coward out of the boot. His bone showing through his worn-out old face. Teeth, tiny chattering things.

The storm raged as I dragged him through the concrete shell. Waves were crashing, wind howling, rain lashing. He struggled, but it was like a child kicking and screaming, clawing at the air.

We reached the marina wall. I held him there, backwards, his centre of gravity already over the water. If one big wave came we would both be swept away.

'Tell me who he is!' I screamed, the wind stealing most of the sound.

I couldn't hear him over the sea crashing against the wall, but I could read 'I can't!' in his lips. His silly shoes slipped on the edge, but I was holding his entire weight with one arm.

'Tell me!'

'He'll kill me!' I actually heard him that time. '*You* won't.'

I felt a chill come over me, far colder than the sea

below us, as I stared deep into his sockets.

'Who told you that?' I said. And I let go.

He slid down the marina wall, trying to find grip, something to stop it happening, but it was no good, and he plunged into the icy water. After a few seconds I saw him surface, but he was caught in a wave and slammed against the wall.

He didn't resurface again.

JOE GRABARZ WILL RETURN IN

CHOOSE YOUR PARENTS WISELY

ABOUT THE AUTHOR

Tom Trott was born in Brighton. He started writing at Junior School, where he and a group of friends devised and performed comedy plays for school assemblies. Since leaving school and growing up to be a big boy, he has written a short comedy play that was performed at the Theatre Royal Brighton in May 2014 as part of the Brighton Festival; he has written a television pilot for the local Brighton channel; and he has won the Empire Award (thriller category) in the 2015 New York Screenplay Contest. He is the proverbial Brighton rock, and currently lives in the city with his wife.

If you have enjoyed this book, please bore everyone you meet at dinner parties, society functions, and bus shelters with how excellent it is. If you have not enjoyed this book, please keep that to yourself.

To purchase this book and others, visit tomtrott.com

For news of upcoming work, follow @tomtrottbooks on Facebook and @tjtrott on Twitter.

43099131R10135

Made in the USA
Middletown, DE
20 April 2019